A SNOW WHITE AND ROBIN HOOD RETELLING

THE FAVORED'S CURSE BOOK ONE

M.K. FELIX

Cover by GetCovers

eBook ISBN: 979-8-9931091-2-1

Paperback ISBN: 979-8-9931091-1-4

Hardcover ISBN: 979-8-9931091-0-7

CONTENTS

For My Husband

Thank you for growing with me.

For encouraging me to become better.

For crying with me, and laughing with me.

You are my forever prince.

READING PROVISIONS LIST

Dear Reader,

To help with your experience reading *Fairest Hunter*, I've gathered a list of provisions for you to acquire, with the hope it'll allow you a truly immersive experience in this book.

Please enjoy the following:

- Roasted Pheasant - A pheasant caught early in the morning (fresh chicken can be a viable substitute) and slow-cooked with a mixture of wild onions and mushrooms from beyond the castle walls, along with potatoes and carrots from the castle gardens

- Apple Turnover - Made with fresh-milled flour, hand-churned butter, a dash of sugar, and apples picked from the village orchards

- Dale's Mystery Stew - Meat chunks (whatever is on hand), along with in-season vegetables. Season with fresh herbs and spices

- Dale's Root Vegetable Stew - Potatoes, ham, maybe a little cream if you happen to have milked a cow recently, seasoned with herbs from the garden

- Fresh Peaches - If magically spelled for more energy and better nutrients, you're lucky. If not, well, I guess you need the merry men to visit your orchards
- Breakfast Porridge – Somehow, it's better than you'd think. Best not to question it. Just add an extra dose of fruit or nuts and pray Dale has woven his magic into it
- Villager's Sweet Rolls - Whatever type of bread you have on hand, just make sure to add a drizzle of honey to the top so Marius will sing you praises
- A Duchess's Tea Party - Petite cucumber sandwiches served on porcelain plates, with sides of sliced meats and cheeses accompanying a fluffy roll
- Chocolate Pudding - Made with the best cream, chocolate, and the secret ingredient the cook won't tell you about, but you don't care because you haven't had chocolate in months
- Breakfast Tray - Bread slices, cheese of choice, and fruit of choice. Make sure it's not poisoned, though

Kingdoms of Miraveil
Fideva
Minela
Garia
Wilia
Laria
Sorila
Uxia
Rovia
Peiria
Sherwood Forest
Lyriva

Chapter One

A Meal Most Unfortunate

Rowena

The king's voice drones on as if we have all the time in the world. In reality, Cook is boiling over because it's an hour into dinner and they haven't started the first course. I see her peek through the servant's entrance again, rolling her eyes before she moves out of my line of sight.

Just another reason why King Ferdinand is not to be trusted. He can't stop talking long enough to enjoy the freshly baked pheasant I shot today, and if tasty fowl isn't worth being silent for, I don't know what is.

My back aches as I lean against the stone wall, the dark leather of my huntress uniform helping me blend in with the guards. Why I'm even here is a question I'm sure we're all asking, but the king's whims are not to be questioned if you value your sanity. He's never called me to a banquet before. Our interactions are usually behind closed doors.

My eyes dart from the head of the table where the king stands, down to the seat next to him. Prince Alvor sits there with a pleasant smile on his face, a vacant look in his eyes, and the same expression I've seen on his face for the past five years when I've caught glimpses of him. His father rambles on about the state of the kingdom, and yet Prince Alvor is absolutely still, not seeming to care that he can't eat until his father is finished speaking.

None can eat until the king sits and takes the first bite—a ridiculous rule, in my opinion.

The food is going to be cold, and the servants will be blamed for it when it's his own kingly heinie's fault.

But who am I to urge the king to stuff his mouth with food I worked hard to procure early this morning? I'm a nobody. A lowly hunter, the only one left, and I only have this job because Father didn't have a son. Father realized I liked weapons and trained me to be his replacement, and I've bested everyone in archery contests who have come to compete to replace me.

Although if Father were still here, he'd never let me touch a weapon if he knew how much more I do besides hunt fowl for the king.

My gaze is drawn back to Prince Alvor, a man I've ignored for years. Yet tonight, my magic tugs at me. A ripple of shock runs through me when Prince Alvor's blue eyes stray from staring into space. They meet mine across the room.

My magic leaps in my chest, and my legs twitch, the desire to step closer to the prince winding my body full of tension. Prince Alvor stares, his gaze unwavering. My magic lurches again. The light swirls like a warm, comforting fire through my veins. I tamp down the innate desire to use it. What would I use it on? There are no animals in the room, my normal affinity, and I can see everyone with my eyes, so I don't need to see the light of their souls to see where they are.

Why is my magic being drawn to Prince Alvor?

Why is it reacting *now*, when I need to hide it from King Ferdinand?

I fist my hands at my side. I don't know, and I don't care, and why is the prince still staring at me? I'm not one of the flirty maidens willing to swoon over the ridiculous man-child.

I mentally yell at Prince Alvor to look away, to do *something* to draw the attention away from me.

But he doesn't. He tilts his head, his eyes boring into me from across the room.

Well, if he won't look away, neither will I.

Against my will, my magic spreads, warming my whole body, urging me to move toward Prince Alvor.

How odd.

Prince Alvor blinks, his mouth twitching, and finally he breaks my gaze, redirecting his gaze down to his lap. His head shakes, as if he could hear my silent, berating humor tingeing his lips. When he lifts his head, he looks at his father, his brow furrowing as he studies the odious man.

Ice rushes through me when Prince Alvor clears his throat.

King Ferdinand glares at him, but Prince Alvor doesn't look away from his illustrious father. "My king, I believe our meal is ready."

King Ferdinand's mouth snaps shut, his cheeks reddening. His blackened stare travels from one noble to the next, to each nobleman and courtier. They wilt under his gaze, and if they haven't already pasted on the permanent vacant expression that plagues the nobility—it's on their faces now.

The same expression that's plagued Prince Alvor for years ... until a moment ago.

Prince Alvor's shoulders are thrown back, his posture straight and proud. Wait—that vapid smile is plastered on his face again. What happened to the smirk and the light in his eyes? The current look on his face, a passive smile, just makes me want to punch him.

Wow, lots of violent thoughts this evening.

King Ferdinand slams his fist on the table, rattling the dishes. "If you desire to eat over listening to the king, then so be it." He sits down so forcefully that his chair rocks backward before slamming back onto the stone floor. The violent crack causes several ladies to gasp, their tall hairdos wavering and tilting to the side.

Just another fashion choice dictated by a king who, I swear, is not in his right mind. After one comment on the attractiveness of a woman's hair piled high, suddenly the entire court decided voluminous columns of hair were to become the mark of beauty. How easily they cower before a king who has proclaimed to be on the lookout for his next queen, yet flits through noblewomen, twisting them to his whims with nary a care in the world.

A boy emerges from the servant's entrance, a covered plate in hand. He slinks to the king's side, places the food down, and lifts the cover before making his quick escape. Unlucky chap must have messed with something in Cook's kitchen to have scored serving the king tonight. No one wants to serve him; his volatile temper is most often taken out on the young servant boys and squires.

The floodgates of serving boys open, delivering plates to the court. The sweet scent of pheasant breast drenched in red wine, with mushrooms and roasted vegetables, assaults my nose. No one lifts a fork, waiting for the king's signal to begin eating.

Just as King Ferdinand lifts his fork to his mouth, my stomach clenches. A mewling sound echoes through the quiet room.

I don't move. I stare at the back of a nobleman's chair. But I feel their gazes, anyway. The guards turn toward me, and I even see Prince Alvor's head tilting in my direction.

I would rather die than admit my stomach made that sound.

Little John was right. I haven't been eating enough. I should really pack something to snack on for my hunting days. The days when I avoid being in the king's employ, I'm able to forage more.

But how am I supposed to stomach eating food that could go to the refugees who find us in Sherwood Forest? Especially when I can flit down to the kitchen after dinner and poach leftovers from Cook before she throws them out—by order of the king.

No. Stomach grumbling aside, our people need the food more than I do. I'll forage to survive, even if looks of disdain over normal bodily functions are my penance.

At least I go hungry for a good cause—not because of a ridiculous king who doesn't realize he's a tyrant over everything, including meals.

The guards who turned to look at me sneer, and it's almost an improvement to their perpetual grumpy-looking faces.

Throughout the first course I subtly shift on my feet, alleviating the tension in their arches. My thin leather boots are made for hunting and silence, not for comfort while standing on stone floors.

The first course is finished, and I sigh as the second is brought out. Only one more to go, if the king is being reasonable tonight. Maybe I was called here on nothing more than a whim of the murderous king? Nope, that's probably just wishful thinking.

"Huntress, attend me." The king's voice rings out across the table. Forks still, and so does the beating of my heart.

For as much as I hate King Ferdinand, and even though I'm secretly rebelling against him, I have yet to conquer the innate reaction his voice brings when he addresses me.

My heart thuds painfully against my chest, urging me to break free. My magic recoils, drawing into me and making itself small inside my chest.

Without the warmth of my magic coursing through me, I grow cold. Frozen in place.

Only a nudge from the sneering guard next to me breaks me out of the trance.

My steps are measured as I resist the urge to flee from this room. Mentally, I'm counting each of my hidden weapons. There are the ones tucked up my sleeve, the dagger tied to my thigh hidden under my hunting leathers, plus the thin one in my pocket lining. If King Ferdinand tries anything—I'm prepared both to fight, and to lose my life. I'm willing to take the odious man down with me if he tries any funny business. I'm not a maid he can dally with and send away when his pleasures are satiated.

My fingers clench, the leather of my gloves creaking. I need to oil them again before I go hunting. The thought brings back a sense of normalcy, and my magic unties itself enough to send a little more warmth and confidence throughout my body.

I stop three feet from the king's chair and bow low, as expected, before straightening. "Yes, King Ferdinand?"

The king's eyes are darkness personified, but they aren't looking at me—they're looking at Prince Alvor. "I find that I have neglected my son's education. If he is to be king one day in the far future, then I need him to learn the art of ... silence. I'd like you to take him on a hunt and *teach* him how to be silent."

My breath catches, and my palms sweat in my gloves, his implied message being communicated clearly. Slowly, I let the air flow out of my nostrils, forcing my heartbeat to steady. It's sheer willpower that keeps my knees from quaking. "Yes, my king. When shall I take him?"

At this, the king finally meets my gaze. His once-brown eyes are black, swirling with a darkness that goes beyond mere hatred. "Tomorrow. He *must* learn, tomorrow."

My carefully laid plans have gone up in flames. With one simple word, everything I've worked for is ruined.

Tomorrow, I'm expected to kill the prince—on the day I had planned to assassinate his father.

Chapter Two

A Father Most Evil

Alvor

Rowena's eyes meet mine, my father's words replaying in my mind as their meaning slowly comes into focus.

I blink, a fog lifting from my thoughts, as if I'm waking up from a long sleep.

My gaze moves down the table, the courtiers' gazes avoiding mine. Father's words must mean more than what he simply said. My stomach twists as memories flit together to paint a clear picture of what's happening.

Father wants me dead.

The thought is like a knife shoving itself into my sternum, twisting as my reality shatters.

Rowena's brown eyes with flecks of green stare me down. My toes move in my dress boots, tapping against the hard soles without making a noise as I hold the rest of my body still.

I wrestle with the thoughts flooding my mind. I cling to the clarity, a sensation that seems to be so foreign. A sharp pain grows in my chest, stoked by the fire flaming through me at the thought that my own father wants me dead.

The longer I look at Rowena, the more I realize it's true. A new thought enters my mind. If Father wants me dead, then has he been sending off noblemen and other courtiers to die? Has he been using Rowena as his own personal assassin?

My nails dig into my palms as I fist my hands in my lap.

Why am I just *now* realizing this?

My heart sinks into my stomach. How many times has Father told Rowena to take someone on a hunt, only for them to never return?

My gaze travels up and down the table, noting the subdued nobles and their emotionless reactions. They look as vacant as I've felt—until I looked into Rowena's eyes tonight. Are they quiet because she's here? Do they know her role in my father's court? Is fear keeping their tongues from wagging?

No, Father's monologue about our kingdom's greatness and how we're better than the rest of the kingdoms on the continent got the evening started at a snail's pace and deepened the feelings of lethargy I felt before . . . before I saw Rowena's eyes.

I blink, searching for those eyes that remind me of the rich colors of the forest. She's moved back to the wall and stands next to the guards, conveniently in a spot where I can easily see her between the noblemen's chairs across the table from me.

Another wave of clarity washes through me. Something is wrong with our court.

I say *our* court, but really, it's Father's. The man has not let me make a single decision of consequence in my twenty-two years of life.

I shake my head again, my mind aching as my pulse throbs against my skull.

Father's piercing gaze draws my attention, and I recoil at the darkness swirling in his eyes.

No.

Something is going on, and I'm finally realizing this is wrong. I don't know when that misty darkness took over Father's gaze, but I'm not going to sit here quietly any longer.

If my death has already been decided, I might as well go out with a bang.

My fingers grip my fork, spearing the meat in front of me as I hide my sudden clarity. I take another bite of the tender bird I'm sure Rowena shot this morning. Hopefully, she'll take my life as easily as she does a bird's. A quick shot is all I can pray for.

But I'm not dead yet.

Though Cook is talented, somehow this meat is tasteless and bitter. I swallow the small bite and set my fork down. I turn to the man causing my indigestion. "Father, about that hunting lesson. Surely I can learn silence through some other means? A day spent in the library with no one to speak to, perhaps? An assignment to study our illustrious history?"

Father's lips curl, his eyes darkening.

Why are they darkening?

Have they always done that?

Father shakes his head, his lip curling in a sneer. "No. The forest shall teach you the true *beauty* of silence."

His words flow into my mind, which fogs over. My thoughts slow. I move my hands to my lap, tapping my fingers against my leg. A part of my mind screams, begging to stay focused, to hold on to my lucidity. There's an invisible tug in my chest, and I turn just enough to look into Rowena's eyes again.

It's like drinking cold spring water. A simple glance and my mind clears enough to put the puzzle pieces together. The longer I look into Rowena's eyes, the more the fog lifts, letting my thoughts slip through.

A question I've been meaning to ask my father for years forms in my mind. Whatever he is doing, it's been happening for a while. With Rowena's gaze bringing back my lucidity, I'm able to voice my suspicions. "If we're to speak of beauty, we must at least discuss the mirror gifted to you some years ago. Remind me who gifted it to us?"

Father's eyes flash, and he snarls before slamming his fist on the table. "The mirror is nothing more than a trinket. Why are you asking about a pointless gift? Clearly you are unfit to rule if you're asking ridiculous questions such as these."

I lean back, wiping spittle off my cheek.

Why am I asking about a mirror?

The mirror doesn't matter. It's beautiful. I've been curious about it whenever I see it in my father's rooms, but it's not important. Movement catches my eye, and I turn, intrigued.

Rowena arches an eyebrow, and there's a tug in my chest, and once again, my mind feels as though it's been dunked in a trough of cold water. My thoughts and feelings are coming clearly into focus.

There's a burning in my chest, a frustration begging for an outlet.

Father is somehow distracting me because the mirror *is* important.

I spear Father with my gaze, not willing to back down as I cling to my seemingly fleeting lucidity. "If it's a trinket, then surely we can display it for all to view, seeing as it's of no value to you. I find it quite beautiful myself, and wouldn't mind looking in it daily."

Father shoots to his feet, chair toppling behind him as he slams his hands once again on the table. He knocks over his empty cup of wine, which rolls into my full one. Dark red liquid spills down the center of the table, staining the pristine tablecloth the maids spent hours ironing due to one of Father's whims.

How do I remember that order, but not important things like *why hasn't Rowena spoken to me for five years*? That feels more important than Father's orders to the maids.

Father points at me, spittle flying from his mouth. "Enough of your ridiculous questions and requests. You are an unworthy heir. You will learn to hold your tongue. If you scare off the game tomorrow, it is your meals that shall suffer."

My mind dulls as his words strike me. The hurt that should be there, only a light pain in my heart.

There's a tug in my chest and I lean forward, my body drawn toward her. My gaze meets Rowena's. Her eyes glow, a stark contrast compared to Father's, which swirl with darkness. With her steady focus on me, I'm able to gather my thoughts, breaking through whatever spell Father's words keep putting me under.

My father's words are absurd, and I hold in my indignant laugh even as a part of me wonders where the father of my childhood went—he never spoke to me this way. But the man before me? I can't imagine why he expects me to believe tomorrow is anything but an execution, albeit a silent one. Especially when he's spewing such hateful words my way.

Slowly, I rise from my seat. I gently push back my chair, in opposition of the violent, angry man standing before me. "As you wish, Father. I will take leave for the rest of the evening to practice your request. Enjoy your silent meal."

I turn, and as I reach the door, Father roars, "Everyone is dismissed!"

My mind clouds over as the door closes behind me. Father's last words echo in my mind. I'm only a few steps down the hallway before the scampering feet of the court echo behind me, escaping the wrath of my father.

My father—an evil king.

My stomach twists as I stagger down the hallway, almost tripping over my own feet before the cloudiness returns, soothing my emotions into a tempered state. My feet slow, my thoughts drifting away until I'm reaching for loose threads.

My walk turns into a casual amble as I turn down the hallway toward the library. Might as well read my favorite books before my death. I'll say goodbye to Cook in the morning; she might be the only one to miss me.

A heavy weight presses against my chest, my heart twisting with a sadness that runs deeper than I've felt in quite some time, though the words to describe why elude me.

The hallway grows darker, and the shadows seem to elongate as I dwell on thoughts of tomorrow. I drag my fingers across the tapestries lining the walls as I walk. I skirt around a suit of armor, a memory of filching the sword to practice against Rowena when we were younger flittering to my mind.

I cling to the sweet moment, a memory I haven't revisited in some time.

Father never allowed me to make real friends. The only person who came close was Rowena, and only because our mothers were friends. I tried to befriend the other young knights and noblemen, but there always seemed to be a rift between me and the other men.

The sensible young women no longer approach me at court events, though I can't remember the last time we've had a ball or dance.

Why haven't we had balls? Shouldn't I have been trying to search for a wife?

The thought flits away like a butterfly as I slip into the gallery, my favorite shortcut to get to the library. My boots kick up the dust on the floor, and I pass by the shrouded pictures on the walls. Father forbade entrance to the gallery after Mother's death.

That's one law I've broken daily—I've visited Mother's picture every day since she died.

I pass a tapestry and start my countdown of the portraits leading up to Mother's. Hers is the twelfth portrait, and was added after her death, and next to it is her lady-in-waiting who died with her—portrait thirteen.

There's a whisper of fabric moving behind me, the slight noise halting my steps. I turn to look behind me, only to see a slim hand reaching out from behind the tapestry separating portraits ten and eleven. My jaw drops as the hand grabs my arm, yanking me toward the woven fabric and the darkness behind it. I trip over my feet before I catch my footing.

Getting kidnapped the night before I die? Why not?

My heart skips a beat as I'm pulled into the darkness, down a hallway, and into a dark room.

Why am I just now discovering that there are secret passages and rooms in the castle? Also, why am I not fighting against whoever is dragging me through the dark?

You know what, if they wanted to kill me, they'll just save Rowena from doing the job. I'd rather not have to look into her face as I die anyway, so might as well be killed in this tunnel.

I'm shoved through a doorway into a small room. I flop onto a sofa, banging my head against its wooden frame. A groan escapes my lips. "Ouch, did you have to be that rough?"

A match flares to life, and my kidnapper lights a candle on the mantle. "So sorry for the bump on your head, Your Highness. I'm sure it'll be the least of your worries when I kill you tomorrow."

Her voice, rich as fine chocolate and smooth as water, runs over me.

Rowena.

Chapter Three

A Plan Mostly Hatched

Rowena

Honestly, why does the prince have to be so tall and have such long legs? He takes up half the room in my quarters, and I'm still trying to figure out where to sit while I maintain some semblance of professionalism.

As professional as a meeting where we plan a coup can be, I guess.

Alvor folds his arms, a scowl marring his perfectly symmetrical, pale face as his blue eyes meet mine. "Finishing me off early, are you?"

I roll my eyes and match his stance as I lean against my wall. "As if I'd actually kill you, princeling. We know you're the only hope for this kingdom. Why would I off you in the forest when I need you to overthrow your father?"

His eyebrows raise and he straightens, soles flat on the ground as he leans forward. "Come again?"

I tilt my chin up. "You heard me. Now are you going to help me or not?"

He rubs his hand along his jaw, his skin freshly shaven. A lock of his dark hair flops across his forehead, ruining the picturesque look. "You really think you can take down my father, Rowena?"

My shoulders move of their own accord, the inelegant shrug masking the twisting in my gut that I feel at admitting my plans to the son of the king. "I've already been planning to overthrow your father. It's either that, or live in squalor while he drives this kingdom to ruin by squeezing every penny out of its people. I'm certainly not going to meekly accept my own death at his hands. Are you?"

He glares, those piercing sky-blue eyes doing nothing besides causing me indigestion.

I still haven't gotten a bite of that pheasant.

Stupid princeling.

Something shifts in his gaze as my magic twists inside me—again. It's been acting up all night, and I'm tired of it. I thought it was hunger, but this is something else, and it has to do with the insufferable princeling in front of me.

Alvor shakes his head, rubbing his eyes before looking at me. "You're serious?"

I scoff. "Are you seriously telling me you were going to waltz into the forest tomorrow, fully expecting me to put an arrow through your heart, and just meekly accept your fate? Where's your backbone, princeling? Your courage? Your desire to rewrite your destiny?"

Alvor's lips thin. "Apparently, it's been dead. As far as I can tell, it's been gone since my mother died, and my father turned into an emotionless tyrant who forsook me and insulted me on a daily basis. It only got worse when your father died. So don't act all high and mighty. I'm tired, Rowena. Tired of fighting against a darkness I've been languishing in until tonight, when *you* changed something inside me." He eyes me, eyebrow raised as he inspects my face.

My heart twinges, and I ignore it. We all have sob stories. His just happens to influence our entire kingdom.

"Ha! What did you feel? Attraction for a measly huntress, Prince Alvor? Don't make me laugh." I wave my hand in the air. "I don't know what this darkness is that you're talking about, but you have to move on. You don't have time to be tired. You can take a nap when you're dead. Oh wait, you're not going to be."

He rolls his eyes, folding his arms and leaning back in repose as if he's the ruler of my small room. "Please, tell me how I might serve you, fairest maiden who holds my heart in her hands—figuratively, of course."

I straighten, my hands flying to my hips, and I take up my intimidating stance I use on my merry men. "Drop the mask, Alvor. I want the real you in this discussion, not the passive prince you've been for who knows how long. Leave that fake junk you pull for everyone else. I want the real man."

His eyebrows lower, his shoulders sagging as his perfect posture falls apart. "Rowena, that fake junk is the real me. Pardon me if I don't actually know who I am anymore. I wasn't lying when I said it's as if I'm waking up from a year-long nightmare. So you'll get what you get tonight, and don't throw a fit."

The last line of his impassioned words cuts through my fiery feelings, and I oddly enough feel a laugh bubble up inside me. I shake my head, not letting the bout of humor escape me. "You've been hanging out with Cook for too long, haven't you? You sound exactly like her."

Finally, a small smile breaks through his surly expression. "She's about as bossy as my father, but I like her more because she sneaks me treats."

I knew it! I knew she made the apple turnovers for him. They've always been his favorite. She won't ever let me snitch one.

I purse my lips. "She has to make you sweets—you're the prince."

This time, he rolls his eyes. "You know Cook does what Cook wants, and only bows to my father's whims because she wants to protect the other servants."

I huff. He's right. Cook cornered me about helping Dale escape the king's wrath even though the undercook drove her batty. My band of merry men have been grateful for Dale's cooking skills ever since. Cook really is a sweetheart.

Our conversation lulls, and I take the opportunity to study the man before me. I've avoided Alvor since becoming the huntress, a wise decision in hindsight. Though there's a sharp pain in my chest as my wonderings take me back into the past. As I study Alvor's face, I can see his growth, yet there's still the young boy from years ago, his confidence and attitude rising from the darkness he says he's been trapped in. He studies me too, and it's as if the annoying way he was able to read people and their motives resurfaces again for the first time in years.

I've been wondering how he hid his sensitivity toward others' feelings for so long. It's driven me crazy watching him play dumb as I slunk through the shadows of the castle while watching him from afar.

The Alvor before me isn't driving me up the wall, and I'm not sure how I feel about it.

When the silence becomes a tad too uncomfortable, I blow out a sharp breath. "Let's get down to business, Alvor. You're not dying tomorrow, and I've got plans. Are you in or are you out?"

He purses his lips. "Unless you have hidden magic or know an assassin, I doubt you're going to succeed."

I shrug. "Good thing I do, in fact, have magic, and that I'm practically trained to be an assassin. So, what am I missing to make this succeed?"

His eyes narrow, the light from the candle flickering in their azure depths, beckoning me to stare into them and lose myself in the darkening sky of Prince Alvor's gaze once again.

But I can't.

I won't.

"Show me," he whispers.

How many times can I scoff in front of the prince before I get in trouble? Doesn't matter. He's making ridiculous requests—he deserves a ridiculous reaction.

I scowl. "You know light magic doesn't work that way."

"Actually, I don't." His voice drops. "I never showed any signs of magic, so Father didn't send me to the academy. He said Sorila was too far away, and I didn't need to get to know the rest of the royals from the continent. All I know are the stories I've read in the library. But I guess I should have asked what type of magic you have before assuming you could show me."

I inspect my nails. "Yes, you should have."

Silence reigns, and I let him squirm.

His boot taps the floor. "Well?"

I lean against the wall, crossing my feet at my ankles and folding my arms. "Fine. Here's your quick magic lesson. Magic comes from light. It's literally light magic, but it manifests differently in each person. Some command their magic, while for others it behaves more innately. Only in rare circumstances am I able to command mine. For the most part, my magic manifests by allowing me to see in the dark, help with animals and treat small injuries, and sometimes it warns me of impending danger. That's all I'm going to say."

His eyebrows draw together. "How were you going to use that to overthrow my father?"

I straighten, pushing off the wall. "Great question, but class time is over." I walk over to my dresser and pull out a paper, ink, and a quill. "Tomorrow I'm taking you to my merry men. I'll have to leave quickly to hunt down a boar substitute for you. This letter will ensure they accept you into my camp. They'll take care of you until I return."

"Your merry men? What does that mean?"

My quill scratches, a soothing sound as I write a few sentences of an inane love note, hiding my keywords only Little John or Red will understand. "There is more to me than you know, princeling. This is just one of my many secrets. Now, who in the court is your least favorite woman vying for your hand in marriage?"

"Lady Marian," he spits out without pausing to think. "She's the only woman willing to approach me, but that girl drives me crazy. I know she's young, and barely part of the court, which earns her my pity, but someone seriously needs to take her under their wing and help her learn to read the room and realize I'm not falling for her—ever."

I chuckle. "Strong feelings, I see."

He runs his hand through his hair, mussing the perfectly styled locks as he groans, exasperation written across his face.

I laugh and turn back to the letter, signing it with Marian's name, and an extra special flourish. I grab my container of sand, sprinkling it on the page before turning back to Alvor.

"After the letter dries, I'm sneaking you back into your room. You'll pack a bag with two changes of clothes and anything else you deem essential for living in the woods for who knows how long. I'll take it and sneak it to where I'm taking you. Go about your life as normal tonight, and tomorrow morning, we'll leave after breakfast. Can't deprive you of one last meal from Cook, or she'll tan my hide."

He shakes his head, studying the wall we entered through, which happens to be opposite the real door in my room. "I didn't even realize we had secret passages."

I shrug. "It's a secret kept by the hunters. There's a whole backstory to it that my father told me once, but now is not the time. Just know it's a secret, and I think I might be one of the last to know about it, and I'd like to keep it that way."

There's a flicker in his eyes, and it's not from the candle. "You're really doing this? Defying my father's orders?"

"Isn't the first time, princeling," I say as I pour the sand back into the container, closing its lid and sticking the letter in my pocket. "And it definitely won't be the last."

Chapter Four

A Hunt Most Silent

Alvor

I bite down into the crisp apple turnover Cook gave me, savoring the sweet pastry. Who knows when I'll have another one of these?

It's been a normal morning, which has me shaking with fury. Because a normal morning in recent years means no one talks to me besides those whom I trained with earlier, and Cook when she gives me food.

The castle is unnaturally silent; the only place where there is a modicum of noise is here in the kitchen, and only then it's the barest conversations.

What has Father done to us all?

Why has no one realized or protested the disappearance of so many people at Rowena's hands? Why haven't I done anything about it?

It's as if my discussion with Rowena last night finally woke me up from a deep, dark slumber. I've been disconnected from reality while still living in it. My morose thoughts of yesterday—how I calmly accepted my own death sentence—feel shocking in the light of day.

Fire burns in my chest, indignation spurring me to move and do something about this horrible life I've simply accepted.

But now it's too late.

At least, it's too late to change things from inside the castle.

Wherever Rowena is taking me promises to be nothing like what I've known in my life so far, and the prospect of the change is thrilling.

I take another bite of my turnover, the soft apples and a dash of cinnamon coating my tongue with their sweetness. Food tastes richer this morning, and my life, well, it's as if I'm living it again. Verbally sparring with Rowena last night was the most alive I've felt in . . . I can't remember how long. Not only because she was someone to match wits with, but because I actually *felt* things. The emotions were tangible and caused *real* reactions within me. I couldn't resist baiting her and battling with words.

Not to mention that spark of attraction. I never thought I'd feel attracted to a woman who dripped disdain as she talked to me.

My life is full of surprises these days.

The last bite melts in my mouth, and I quickly lick the tips of my fingers, making sure I get every single bit of flaky crust.

Cook walks over to my side, a kind smile on her lips emphasizing the wrinkles at the corner of her eyes. "Need another turnover, Prince Alvor?"

My stomach grumbles, not fully satiated by the sweetness. "Maybe one for the road? Rowena asked me to meet her after I finished eating. I should bring one for her too."

Cook's eyebrows lift, but that's the only thing she says as she bundles up two turnovers, four rolls, and a wedge of cheese, handing me the wrapped cloth. "Best get on your way. She's an impatient little thing." Cook clucks her tongue and nods toward the door. But I'm not ready to say goodbye yet.

I walk around the counter and wrap my arm around her shoulder, pulling her into a hug and breathing in her cinnamon-sugar scent. "Thanks, Cook. For everything."

She swats my back before leaning into my embrace. "Aw, best get on with you, boy. Before you make me ruin this dough with my salty tears."

I give her one last squeeze before exiting the kitchen doors. The gardens look greener today, the sky brighter and air cleaner than it had been in years. The blooming flowers woven between the vegetables bring a cheerfulness belaying the circumstances of the day. The pathway to the gate leading toward Sherwood Forest is well worn, the gate hinges silent as I push it open.

The guards are silent, eyeing me as I walk away from the castle. Little do they know—or maybe they do know—I won't be coming back.

Rowena leans against a tree trunk, arms crossed, her hood up so her face is unreadable from where I am. All except her mouth, which is firmly set. Her eyes are shadowed, yet I still can feel her stare burning into me.

Her hunting leathers show off her lean figure, her quiver full of arrows poking out from behind her hood, along with the tip of her bow. Instead of the long leather tunic, she's wearing a jerkin, leather pants with knives strapped to the outsides of her thighs, and knee-high boots.

Rowena's outfit is lethal—and not just to those animals she hunts. My heart races as I approach her, manifesting the risk of spending time with this deadly huntress.

"Ready to go, princeling?" She pushes off the tree, not waiting for my answer as she walks through the gate.

Rowena is silent as we trek through the forest. We only stop once to grab the pack I made last night, which I throw over my shoulder. Then off we go again.

The trees grow thicker the farther we travel until she leads us to a small deer trail. The trail thins as the woods grow taller, yet branches still whip me in the face as I pump my legs, trying to keep up with the leaping gazelle that is my guide.

Rowena's shorter stature gives her an advantage as she darts through the woods. I never thought I'd be jealous of our height difference. But after another tree smacks me, cutting my cheek, the sting of the wound wakes me up to another reality.

I may be good with a sword, but my footwork, stealth, and stalking abilities are laughable.

No, wait—Rowena is actually laughing. Of course she is.

She slows enough to speak to me over her shoulder. "You could always bend over a bit, or stick your arm out to push the branches out of the way."

I puff out a breath. "Rowena, you're practically galloping through these woods. Keeping up with you requires all my stamina and focus. I can't watch for roots that will trip me while keeping an eye on branches that are going to take my head off."

She shakes her head, laughing as she continues to jog ahead of me as if she's done this every day of her life, instinctively dodging branches and lifting her feet higher when a particular tree root blocks the path. "Definitely can't have you die prematurely. It'd ruin my reputation. But don't worry, princeling, we're almost there."

I suck in a breath. "Where?"

Rowena doesn't answer; instead, she slips her fingers into her lips and trills a whistle. Only a second later, and we hear an answering trill a distance ahead of us. Rowena nods. "Good, John will be there to meet you."

My eyebrows draw together as I heave out my next words between my gasping breaths. "Who is John?"

Rowena takes mercy on me and slows her steps. "One of my merry men."

I raise my hands, placing them behind my head as I work to control my breathing. "How many merry men do you have?"

Rowena shrugs as she looks around through the trees. "Six officially, but many more unofficially who have joined our wee band of outlaws."

I raise my eyebrows. "Outlaws?"

She turns back to me. "Have a problem with that, princeling?"

I shrug. "Depends on what your definition of outlaw is."

She arches an eyebrow, laughter lining her eyes. "You're one now too, you know. Anyone who defies the king's orders is an outlaw. The only difference is that my men and I have decided not to be passive about our rebellion."

Pieces click together in my head, emerging from the dull darkness of the past few years. Memories of whispers between noblemen come together, forming a clear picture of just who Rowena is. Rumors of robbing, disappearing villagers, and second sons rebelling against their parents, all point to one thing—or rather person.

My hands drop, my shoulders sagging. "Rowena, please tell me you aren't who you're saying you are."

Rowena tilts her head up, her hood falling back enough to be able to look into her grinning face. "Can't do that, princeling. That'd be *lying.*"

There's that odd tug in my chest, and I resist the urge to get closer to the intriguing woman before me. My mind clears again, as it has been doing when in Rowena's company. This is another secret Father has wanted to keep hidden, why he stopped the nobleman from loitering around and gossiping. He doesn't want the news of the bandits to spread ... especially not the mention of Robin Hood.

A branch snaps behind Rowena, and she rolls her eyes. "Come on out, Little John."

She pulls the letter she wrote last night from her pocket and slaps it against my chest. My hand comes up to grip it, brushing against her gloved fingers.

She yanks her hand back, pulling her hood back up and over her face. "Give this to my men. They'll take care of you."

Then she bounds away like a rabbit, hopping and sprinting down the trail toward the castle.

"Come back here, Robin!" a man shouts as he steps from behind a wide oak tree farther up the trail.

He towers over my six-foot frame, and his shabby brown hair, the same color of his leather tunic, adds to the intimidation factor. He's built like an ox, with muscles from his neck to his toes. How he walked so silently is a mystery.

"Um, hi," I mutter, my hand crinkling the letter Rowena gave me as I continue to hold it against my chest.

The big man—I'm assuming he's Little John, which would be just like Rowena to name him based on his stature—folds his arms, glaring at me. "So you're Robin's newest stray?"

I arch an eyebrow. "Robin? Do you mean Rowena?"

Little John frowns. "In the woods, she is Robin. Makes it less confusing for the new people who don't know her real identity, and it's less likely her escapades will be whispered about back to the castle folk. From now on, she's Robin to you."

My throat goes dry, but I'm a little sick of being bossed around today. "What happens if I call her Rowena?"

He takes a menacing step forward. "You don't want to know. Now hand me that letter."

My arm snaps out, dropping the offending paper in his hand as I tamp down the desire to pick an argument with the hulking man. Little John unfolds the parchment, scanning the words before a deep laugh rumbles out of his chest. "Oh, Robin, of course you did."

I fold my arms. "Did what?"

John's green eyes meet mine. "She saved your life, Prince Alvor, and now she's going to help you take it back."

I shake my head. "But how? She just ran away."

He nods. "It takes her a long time to hunt down the wild boars. Your father has hunted them to near extinction for sport, but they're the most similar to a human heart and the most convincing. She takes their hearts to your father who is none the wiser."

My stomach churns, and I swallow down the bile burning my throat. "My father wants their hearts?"

John nods. "Not sure why. He's plumb crazy that one is—no offense, Your Highness."

I huff out a laugh. "None taken, particularly because I agree."

I run my hands through my hair before gripping the straps of my travel bag we picked up from a hiding spot Rowena made for supplies just inside the forest. She must have hidden it there last night. Did she even sleep? And now she's going hunting?

John starts walking. I fall into step behind him. "So, John. What is it that Rowena has you do?"

"Her name is Robin," he mutters before pushing a branch out of his way. I'm just fast enough to catch it before it smacks into me.

Little John grunts. "Come see what we do, Prince Alvor. Be prepared—you're about to meet your poorest subjects."

I follow him another hundred yards before noises start filtering through the trees. Laughter, children squealing with happiness, and muted conversations reach my ears before the trees fade away and I step into an encampment. A sea of tents, with a few log buildings, greets me. But no one else does. Instead, conversations cease, and hushed whispers ripple through the crowd.

John steps forward, his voice booming. "Everyone, come meet Prince Alvor—our newest outlaw."

Chapter Five

A Heart Most Dead

Rowena

My knife cuts through the flesh with precision. I sharpened the blade this morning while waiting for Prince Alvor to finish his breakfast. The man sure did take his time.

I send up a silent prayer as I work on cleaning the boar at my feet.

This hunt has weighed on me all day, my magic seemingly displeased by how I used it today. My magic works in mysterious ways, and though there is a magic academy I could have attended, Father kept my magic a secret. I'm sure there's logic to how my magic works, and I've discovered some of it on my own, but most of it remains a mystery to me.

Connecting with animals is easy—at least the domesticated ones. I intrinsically know their wants, joys, and pains. They understand me on a deeper level. Which is why I can sense an injured animal from several miles away.

But some I can't sense. The wilder ones, the ones set on destruction—they're harder to track, and I'm forced to rely on age-old hunting skills passed down from generations of royal hunters.

The boar took me on a wild chase over the course of the morning after dropping Prince Alvor off with John. The sun is burning in the sky, only the shade from the copse of trees giving me some reprieve from its intense heat.

I'm too far north to take any of it back to the encampment. But there is a village nearby. The butcher has a hand wagon, and if I play my cards right, he can quietly distribute the meat amongst the poorest villagers.

But first, I pull out the wooden box from my pack. It's lined with leather, stained from years of use, and makes my stomach revolt every time I look at it.

I drop the boar's heart in the box, closing it and securing the latch, before putting it in another leather bag in my pack. My movements are rehearsed, something I've done so many times it's a habit, which is how I avoid thinking about having taken the poor boar's life.

I kill animals to survive, not because I like it. With my magic, I can choose the animals I kill, thus maintaining Mother Earth's cycle of life and death, maintaining a balance that others overthrow.

The meat in front of me means I can't hide in the forest all day, even though I want to. It's two hours back to the castle from this part of the forest, and I'd rather catch the king after the evening meal. I do not want to be a spectacle of his court for a second night in a row.

I pull the boar to the foot of a wide tree and cover it in branches—not that the camouflage will do much good against predators, but it'll at least be hidden until I can send one of the villagers to retrieve its carcass.

I follow the descent of the sun to the small village of Roarkly. The butcher answers my quiet knock on his back door and agrees to retrieve the boar. Per my request, he agrees to distribute the meat to the young families first. It's not the first time I've met the middle-aged man, and his soft heart does him credit. He'll become a village elder in no time.

I slink through the shadows of the village until I meet the main road leading south to the castle. Best start running if I want to make it on time. Plus, Red is always lapping me during our exercises. I need to work on my stamina.

I hate running. Running is for fools.

My legs feel like gelatin after racing through the forest, and then back to the castle. I haven't run like this in one day in a *very* long time.

The prospect of looking disheveled in front of the king has my stomach turning. I'll be putting on the act of a lifetime as I give him the supposed heart of his son. But there's nothing to be done about my haggard appearance now that the guards have already spotted me.

They nod their heads as I stroll through the side gate of the castle. I never go through the front. The ornate iron gates gracing the entrance of the castle are for the people who want to posture—or for servants who don't know any better.

Plus, the side is where you can sneak into the kitchens. Cook is the *only* good thing about this place.

I sneak into the kitchen entrance, keeping to the walls and avoiding the subdued servants. I grab one sweet roll from a basket on the corner of a table before slipping down a side corridor. There's a tapestry leading into the secret hallways here. My need to avoid other humans is at an all-time high tonight. I don't have the mental capacity to put on a brave face and make small talk.

I pause at the edge of the corridor, taking a bite of the sweet roll as I wait for the servant to turn the corner. Their footsteps fade, and I slip beneath a tapestry of a long-forgotten war between Solwain and the darkness plaguing the land.

I keep the doors of the secret passageways well maintained, and this one slides open with the quietest click of the metal latch. My steps are silent, and with my magic I don't need a torch to guide my way; the shadows are bare whispers of darkness thanks to the warm magic coursing through my veins.

I travel up a dusty set of stairs to the royal family's corridor. I slide open the door and wait behind the tapestry. It's silent. I mentally reach inside me, begging for a dash of magic to use. It leaps and bounces, like a rabbit ready to play, and I send out a mental wave of light, searching for heartbeats of humans or animals in the vicinity.

In my mind a mental image creates itself, layering over the map of the castle. No humans in this hallway, though there are two guards and a person who I'd assume is the king in his chambers around the corner.

Perfect.

I slip out, closing the door and letting the tapestry fall into place with a bare whisper.

My knees quiver, and I flex my muscles to stop the reaction. My feelings? They're going in a locked box in my mind.

I will be stiff.

I will be emotionless.

I will not let a single thought or feeling slip through my mask.

I am the huntress, and King Ferdinand doesn't know who he has messed with.

With all the confidence I can muster, I walk down the hallway and stand between the two guards flanked on either side of the king's door. My knuckles rap on the hard wood, the hollow sound reverberating through the empty hallway.

"Come in."

Just the sound of King Ferdinand's voice makes my skin crawl.

The metal handle is cold in my grip as I push the door open. There the man sits on his gold-plated sofa, a writing desk on his lap. His eyes are on the parchment in front of him as gold coins slip through his fingers, clinking into the pouch at his side.

My eyes roam over the space, taking an inventory of the room. No guards, no women. Just a bed, his sofa, a desk, and a large gilded mirror against a wall.

Wait—

I've never seen it uncovered. I thought it was a portrait of Prince Alvor's mother that was shrouded due to grief.

My heart skips a beat. Didn't Prince Alvor mention something about a mirror at dinner last night?

The warmth of my magic, my constant companion, cools inside of me as I stare at the ornate oval mirror. The longer I look at it, the darker the room gets, and it's almost as if shadows seep from its edges, leaking from the mirror to the floor, inching toward me.

"Ahem." The king clears his throat, and as I blink, the darkness disappears, the room looking as it normally does.

I whip my head back toward the king, giving him my full attention. He raises an eyebrow, and I finally remember what I'm supposed to deliver.

The small pack on my back easily comes off, and I crouch down, pulling out the evil box nestled inside. I tug at the leather covering until only the box sits in my hands, and I extend my hand to King Ferdinand.

He trembles as he delicately grabs the box. He lifts the lid, an evil smile warping his face. "You have done well, my little huntress. I knew you'd understand my instructions. You may leave."

He sets the box down and waves his hand, shooing me toward the door. His eyes immediately zero in on the ledger before him, his fingers finding their way back into the bag of coins. How the man can be so callous as he sits there believing I handed him his son's heart as he counts the gold stolen from his subjects is beyond mortal comprehension.

I click the heels of my boots together and do an about-face. The sooner I leave this room, the less likely I am to pull out my hunting dagger and plunge it into the king's own heart.

But I didn't plan on killing the king with a weapon today. Nope. The black leaves of the fairy's death are tucked into the hidden compartment in my boot's heel. The poisonous leaves are something found only deep in the forest, and only if you know where to look for them.

His drink of choice tonight would have been his downfall.

Except, saving Alvor today changed things.

It would have been easier to execute an assassination with Alvor in favor.

But would that have fixed whatever darkness is plaguing our kingdom?

I take a final glance at the mirror. Dark tendrils of mist float across the floor toward me. It must be a cursed object.

So *that's* why Alvor asked about hidden magical abilities.

I push open the door, walking past the guards into the empty hallway. I check to ensure I'm alone before slipping beneath the tapestry. The door closes behind me, and I lean against the wall in the cramped space, letting myself cry.

This coup just got a lot more complicated.

Chapter Six

A Night Most Long

Alvor

I had zero expectations of how the rest of my life was going to go, but this was not on the list of possibilities this morning when I thought about it.

The log beneath me is rough, and I've shifted several times, attempting to find a more comfortable position. But with every small movement, Stue side-eyes me, so I stay put as I watch the spectacle unfold before me. Young men are wrestling in a makeshift dirt arena outside the eating area as children and adults cheer them on, yelling loudly when their favorite competitor earns a point or makes a particularly cunning move.

My hands clap woodenly along with everyone when the round ends. It's been a long day, and honestly, I just want to sleep. But I can't tear my eyes away from everything and everyone around me.

For one, Rowena's crew decided that today I need to be shown the best of the best when it comes to Rowena's—I mean Robin's—encampment.

I've seen the huts, tents, archery range, paddocks, goat pens, vegetable gardens, and now everyone's fighting skills.

Except Rowena's, because she's not back yet. There's a niggling worry in the back of my mind that's grown into an insatiable itch the longer she's gone. Why am I worried about her after she abandoned me here without a word of when she'll return?

I don't know ... but I'd like to see a familiar face here.

That's a lie. There are two familiar faces here; I just don't want to see them. They're not as pretty as Rowena, for one. Second, one of them is currently glaring at me, and I'm over it. Third, well, the guilt is eating me up from the inside out, which is an uncomfortable experience.

The next wrestling match ends by the time I work up the nerve to say something to Little John, who sits at my side. "Little John, can you please tell William Scarlett to stop glaring at me?"

Little John scoffs and shakes his head. "You have two legs and a mouth. Walk over there and tell him yourself. I'm not your lackey."

I tap the heel of my boots in the dirt, biting back a retort. Little John is right, though. I need to talk to William, and then to Marius, if I want to stop this nauseating heaviness pounding against my chest. My heart beats in a rhythm that reminds me that I'm the bad guy, or at least related to the truly evil person. I mean, I probably am the bad guy, because for who knows how long, I haven't cared who Father sent to their death.

Seriously, how have I not cared that he's turned into an evil man? What happened to the father of my youth?

My nails dig into my palms as I clench my fists before loosening them and slapping them against my thighs. "I'm going, then."

Little John nods, his gaze drawn back to the new opponents, two scrawny teenage boys who are more bone than anything else. I'll be glad to not watch this one. Their prominent rib cages are a reminder of my father's insatiable greed.

I walk around the dying cook fire, the smoke stinging my eyes as I approach William. He stares me down as I stop in front of his log bench. Conveniently, there's a space open by his side. I'd hazard a guess that the death glare he's been sending me all evening scared off any potential company. But I'm not going to wilt under the eyes of the man whose same blood runs through my veins.

I sit down, leaning forward until my elbows rest on my knees, staring at the dying coals in front of us. "Hello, cousin."

He grunts. "Why are you here, Alvor?"

I shrug. "Same as you. I questioned my father, spoke out of turn, and he decided I wasn't worth keeping alive."

He leans forward, matching my stance, though his shocking red hair falls across his face, the main physical difference between us. He spits into the dirt. "So the prince with his head in the clouds has more of a spine than I thought."

I tilt my head. "What do you mean 'head in the clouds'?"

William turns toward me, his eyebrows arched, disdain dripping from his words. "You've cared about no one and nothing concerning our kingdom in years. Rumor is your head is up in the clouds. I started to think it was because of misplaced pride and vanity." He looks me over. "Maybe I was wrong."

I hang my head, the harshness of his accusation washing over me. The problem is—he's not wrong. I lift my head and look into his eyes. "William, can I be honest? I don't know what's been wrong with me. But yesterday, I saw Rowena, and suddenly I could think again. My mind has been clearer ever since she spoke to me. I have no excuses for not trying to save you. I know you were right about the trade agreement, and for calling Father a tyrant. That's what he is. You didn't deserve to die for speaking your mind."

His lips thin. "I didn't."

I nod. "I know. I'm guessing Rowena has been saving those sent to be executed for the past few years?"

William nods. "That's mainly who makes up this camp. Survivors of the king's wrath. Or those who can't survive under your father's newest batch of taxes."

I groan. "He raised them again?"

William scoffs. "He raised them two weeks ago. Sent out guards to collect, and those who couldn't afford it lost more than just their money, Alvor. He's killing our people—killing our kingdom—for his greed."

My stomach churns. "How many?" I rasp.

He grunts. "Two hundred over the last five years."

I lean forward, my head between my knees, my hands in my hair as I gasp for air.

Two hundred of my people—gone. Two hundred needlessly killed because of my father's avarice.

It's too much. Guilt gnaws at me. The fact that I'm breathing while others have stopped weighs on my shoulders, dragging me down.

"Red! What have you done to him?" Rowena's voice hisses close to my head.

William shifts next to me, but I keep my head down, barely able to follow the conversation while battling the darkness in my mind and heart.

"I told him about the atrocities his father, the evil king, has committed."

Rowena groans, and then a hand lands on my shoulder. I can sense her next to me, somehow having taken William's spot.

Fingers stroke through my hair, stirring up a warmth in my chest as she whispers in my ear, "Alvor. It's not your fault. I think I know what's happened."

I bring my head up an inch, tilting it so I can look into her entrancing eyes. "It is," I whisper. "It's *my* fault. I could have prevented it. But I. Didn't. Care." I tug on my roots, wishing the pain could distract me from the devastation inside of me. "Why didn't I care, Rowena?"

Her voice is the barest whisper, and I'm not sure I hear her correctly. "You're cursed."

My hands still, and slowly I straighten, the flaying of my heart pausing as I process her words. I stare into her eyes, the hints of green sparkling in the firelight. This close, I can see the smattering of freckles across her nose and cheeks. Her face is serious, her mouth set into a thin line.

"Did you say cursed?"

Rowena's eyes dart to the side before she grabs my hand, pulling me up with her as she stands. "Not here, Alvor. Let's go to my hut. We'll discuss it."

William grunts. "You're not going anywhere alone with him." He spits the words as if I'm poison, and I guess I am, considering how many people have died at the hands of my father.

Rowena rolls her eyes. "Fine. Then come with us, Red. This concerns you and your family as well."

He squints, studying her face before nodding.

Rowena tugs on my arm, pulling me behind her as she leaves the light of the fire. We walk the dark paths of the forest, and I follow without protest because I could have sworn she said I'm cursed.

I need to know what she means—immediately.

Chapter Seven

A Curse Most Dark

Rowena

My grip tightens on Alvor's sleeve as I lead him through camp. We weave through the tents, and my magic floods my system, allowing me to see clearly as we walk deeper into the darkness. My hut is at the edge of camp. It's easier to sneak away when I'm not in the center of the hustle and bustle, plus a woman needs her space sometimes.

My jaw aches from my clenched teeth. The missing pieces of the puzzle concerning King Ferdinand and his unnatural rule have finally been revealed, and the fire burning in my belly has me itching to do something about his evil ways.

If only I were capable of actually killing a person.

The deathly leaves in my boot burn in my conscience. I'll need to dispose of them safely—they're of no use to me now, because I know what Alvor is going to say when I tell him my news.

Alvor and Red stomp across the ground behind me. They're working to keep up with my quick pace and snapping small branches all along the way.

Well, Alvor is snapping branches. The man walks like a bear through the forest; Red at least can sneak.

There's a quiet grunt from Alvor, and only then do I realize I'm digging my fingernails into his arm. I let go and flex my fingers before balling my hands into fists.

I've had my suspicions over the past five years. Things changed when Alvor turned eighteen. The memories haunt me—my father's funeral, being summoned to the king's chamber, receiving instructions to become the new huntress, the king's secret killer.

Father never told me being the hunter meant being an assassin, but now the training I went through when I was younger makes more sense.

My grief was too heavy to protest the king's orders to his face, but the goodness my parents nurtured in me, and the light of my magic, wouldn't let me succumb to his malicious instructions. It feels as if I've been surviving, trying to stay one step ahead in a game I don't even know the rules to.

Little John was my first assignment. I had just turned eighteen when King Ferdinand summoned me to his study, instructing me to take Little John into the forest on the pretense of going on a hunt. Instead, I was to kill him and blame it on a wild animal.

The king wanted his heart as proof.

That father of my friend turned into the evil king, and the innocence of childhood was yanked away from me in a single moment. I could see just how far our king had fallen.

With Little John's help, we hatched a half-baked plan—which it still technically is. This coup we've been discussing for five years keeps falling through with every new order, raised taxes, and supporters who have gone suspiciously complacent toward the king's diabolical plans.

Tonight, everything is going to change, for good—no more excuses.

The fur pelt covering the entry to my hut slips through my fingers as I pull it aside, ushering Alvor and Red inside. Red makes himself right at home, grabbing a candle and lighting it with the flint in his pocket before setting it on the single table in the room. Alvor stands in the middle of the room for a moment, his eyes roving over my meager belongings.

I loosen my grip on the fur as I walk in, letting it fall flat behind me. The cot calls my name, and how I wish I could sleep away these feelings boiling inside me, the oblivion of a dreamless sleep allowing me to momentarily forget everything that needs to be done to fix Lyriva. Red sits on the floor, his back against the far wall, while Alvor seats himself on the singular chair next to my small cooking pot hanging over my cold fireplace.

Alvor's arms are folded, but his leg bounces incessantly, just like it did during lessons with our tutors. He could never stand history class, which was a particular favorite of mine.

"You said I'm cursed."

My fingers find the end of my braid, twisting it as I gather my thoughts. The weight of my anger is distracting, but I need a clear head to explain this well. I suck in a deep breath, slowly letting out the air before I flit my gaze between the two men crowding my small home. "I'm going to start from the beginning. If you interrupt with questions, this will take too long, so save them for the end."

Both men nod, and I scoot back on my cot until my back hits the log wall. I cross my legs and pull my threadbare pillow into my lap, hugging it tightly. Might as well be comfortable while I explain my suspicions.

Blue eyes beckon to me, and I can't help but stare into them as I explain the tapestry of deceit I unraveled as I traveled back from the castle. "Alvor, the king has always been greedy. But when your mother died ten years ago, it began to be a problem."

Alvor leans forward. "When our mothers died in the carriage accident?"

My heart aches and I rub my chest. "Yes." I shoot him a glare as I drop my hand back into my lap. "But that's beside the point. Oh, and don't interrupt me. I've got lots of history to cover."

He nods. "I apologize."

His sincerity earns him a pass this time. "Where was I? Oh yes, your father's greed started to take over. My father was his hunter and an advisor. I imagine it was their friendship that kept the king in check. Father died five years ago, and by the time I realized what was happening . . . it was too late."

"You were grieving," Alvor whispers.

I huff, squeezing my pillow tighter. "And you'll be grieving your life if you keep interrupting me. This isn't about me. This is about you. So just be quiet and listen."

Red chuckles until I turn my glare on him. He quiets instantly, finding the packed-dirt floor fascinating.

I tug on my braid. "Five years ago, your father was gifted a mirror. I do not remember from whom, but I remember it was from another kingdom. That's when everything changed. People slowly started to not care about each other, especially those living at the castle and part of your father's court. Not only that, but your father has been raising taxes to a ridiculous amount. No one has challenged him about it because they've been in a daze. He's taking money not just from the villagers but his nobles and courtiers. He's charging them per meal they have at the castle, yet no extra money has been given to Cook to buy supplies. All of it is going in his coffers."

There's a quiet growl from the men, but I continue on, not pausing to assuage their anger that matches the red-hot coals burning in my chest. I spear Alvor with my gaze. "Your father has always kept the mirror covered. It wasn't until this evening that I saw it fully. I've never been able to understand the thrall everyone has been under. Well ... not everyone."

My gaze lands on Red, who stands leaning against the far wall.

Red grunts. "It's my magic, isn't it?"

Prince Alvor raises his hand as if we are back in class with our tutors again. My eyes only roll once. "Yes?"

Alvor turns to Red. "William, do you have magic?"

Red nods. "Yup. Just a little bit, but probably enough to resist whatever your father is doing. The king never did like that he didn't have magic. Was always jealous of my mother and me for what little bit we had. Lyriva has never outlawed magic, but seeing as the Academy of Radiance is across the continent, training magic users has never been a priority for our people."

Alvor rubs his jaw, the scratch of the light scruff on his chin cutting through the silence. "I didn't know."

Red shrugs. "How could you? You were next to your father all the time growing up, and especially after the queen died. You didn't see anything other than what the king wanted you to." Red kicks his heel into the dirt. "Plus, you don't have magic. It's hard to understand the struggles when you're not the one dealing with them."

Though Red's words make sense and should offer a measure of comfort, Alvor looks as if he's ready to pick a fight, his blue eyes shimmering in the meager candlelight. The man's jaw is clenched so tightly I'm afraid he's going to crack a tooth.

I clap my hands together. "Focus, boys. Point is, when I saw the uncovered mirror tonight, I saw the corrupted magic. I could sense it. Now that I've seen the darkness emanating from it, I can see it everywhere. It's heavier around the people at the castle. The darkness is fading away from you, princeling. Whatever curse or enchantment people have been under comes from *that* mirror, and your father is wielding it for his personal gain."

Neither man says a word, their expressions firm as they stare at me.

Alvor's brow twitches. "He's been cursing us . . . but is he cursed?"

I shrug. "I don't know. It could have cursed him when he got it, and he's just spreading it. Or he could actually be evil, and it's multiplying the darkness in his heart."

Alvor's face falls, and though my fingers itch to reach out and thread my fingers through his, or grip his shoulders, or do something to ease the pain, I don't.

My gaze turns to the prince's cousin. "Red, your family was sent from court after your actions. But that means they're protected from the curse. All those outside of the castle and the city are free of the darkness, unless they've recently come for a visit."

Red sighs, his shoulders relaxing a fraction.

I tighten my fists. "The curse explains why those with a family history of magic have left court. They either thought they would be the king's next victims, or they sensed what I should have long ago. Our goal has always been to depose the king."

I watch Alvor as his fingers tap out a staccato rhythm on his leg while he stares at the ground. The man's wound tight like a mountain lion, ready to pounce at the slightest movement. The fierceness in his expression reminds me of the Alvor I grew up with—the one who treated me like I was special. Like a friend.

"We can't just kill my father anymore. Can we?" Alvor sighs. His blue eyes meet mine.

I shake my head. "I don't think so. Who knows if the curse is tied to him, or the mirror, or both. The mirror needs to be our top priority now."

Alvor lets out a heavy breath. "And how do we get rid of the curse? Do we even know if I'm cured, or whatever it is, yet?"

I study Alvor's blue eyes, which are brighter than I've seen them in five years. "I don't know if you're cured. I know my magic called out to you, but who knows how much of it lingers inside of you."

Alvor drops his head into his hands, running his fingers through the dark strands. "Why does this have to be so complicated?"

No one answers, and silence reigns as heavily as the evil-cursed man sitting on the throne of our kingdom.

Red leans back, his ankles crossing as he folds his arms. "How do we destroy the mirror?"

A sigh escapes my lips. That's the real crux of the problem. "I don't know. It would help if we knew someone who knew things about curses and such. Know anyone who went to the Academy of Radiance?"

Red runs his fingers through his scarlet curls, creating a frizzy mess of his hair. "Actually, I do. My uncle is a doctor on my family's estate. His magic numbs and takes away pain. I always snuck out to see him when I broke a bone and didn't want my mother to find out. He went to the academy."

I mentally run through my schedule. "Tomorrow Cook is expecting a deer from me. I'll hunt early so we can visit the doctor in the afternoon."

Red nods as he stands up from the floor.

Alvor stands with him. "What do you want me to do until then?"

I shrug. "Make friends, talk to the refugees, clean and organize the camp. Whatever you want to do, princeling. Just be ready by midday tomorrow." I stand up, pushing at their shoulders, urging them out of the door. "Now get out of here. I'm ready to sleep. It's been a *long* two days."

Red laughs, but Alvor stumbles on the dirt as he steps out of my home, turning back to me, confusion written across his face. "Where am I sleeping?"

I fold my arms, leaning against the wall of my home. "Not my problem, princeling."

Red slaps Alvor on the shoulder, making the prince wince. "You can stay in my hut, cousin."

The poor princeling looks like a lost puppy. I hold in my laugh. "Good night, princeling."

He nods. "Night, Row—Robin."

I let the fur swing closed, settling over the door frame. I blow out the candle and let my night vision take over as I ready for bed.

But when I lie down, all I can think about is how I wish Alvor had said my real name. He's the only one who seems to have remembered it—and who I *really* am.

Chapter Eight

A Friend Most Needed

Alvor

I stumble down the dirt path, trailing behind William, or is it Red? What's with everyone and the nicknames anyway?

My mind is overloaded, unsure of what to focus on after everything Rowena told us.

Curses, darkness, distraction, greed—all things no man wants to blame their father for.

How do I reconcile the man I grew up knowing with the king he's become?

"You can't solve anything tonight," William says over his shoulder. "Don't stress. Let's get you a cot and introduce you to the rest of Robin's merry men."

I shake my throbbing head. "I don't think I'm pleasant company tonight, William."

He rubs the back of his neck. "Can you call me Red?"

I arch my eyebrows. "I can try."

He nods. "That's fine. You've met Little John, and you know Marius. Now we need to introduce you to Stue, Dale, and Much."

My eyebrows pull together, trying to remember the names but having them flit away with memories of Rowena's discussion barging back into my mind. "Am I supposed to remember all of their names?"

William chuckles. "Each of us is unique. You won't have any issues knowing who we are."

He stops at a hut, opening the door. He lifts out a folded blanket and hands it to me. "For you. This is our supply shed. When refugees come to camp, they often don't have much. Extra supplies we gain go in here for when someone needs them. My hut is around the corner. You'll bunk with me."

I nod, holding the thin blanket close to my chest. We're nearing the end of spring, when the afternoons can be sweltering, yet the nights still cool quickly. Though my body yearns for the luxury of my bed at the castle, I shove away the idea of complaining. I've been rescued from death. This little blanket is a blessing, and I'll be grateful for its meager warmth.

We turn, following the path around a large stand of trees. A small clearing opens, and I halt when I see the five men sitting on logs ringing a small fire pit. I recognize Little John, Marius, and two men from the wrestling matches earlier. The last one was the cook who surprisingly made the thin stew taste delicious.

"Perfect," William says as he steps over to the last empty log. "Sit down, Alvor. This is our crew. With you joining us, we'll be a band of seven."

Varying levels of acceptance line the faces of the men in front of me. Little John doesn't smile, but he does give a small grunt in greeting.

One man grumbles something and spits in the dirt. It isn't the worst reaction I expected, so I'll take it. Though I've been in front of the court my whole life, this group seems more important—their opinions more significant than any others—except Rowena's.

Marius smiles at me, a grin I remember from many a night when he sang during our meals at the castle. "Welcome, Prince Alvor."

"Thank you, Marius. I'm surprised to hear your greeting."

"Why should you be? 'Twas your father who sent me away to be killed, young prince. Now that you're here, I shall have even more songs to write," Marius says, his grin growing wider until his whole face lights up. His eyes crinkle. "I imagine I'll have plenty of songs to sing about you and our dear Robin in the near future." He wiggles his eyebrows suggestively until an elbow meets his side.

The man beside Marius sneezes and wipes his nose on his sleeve—his frown matches his attitude from a moment ago. My eyes are drawn to the dark spot in the dirt at his feet. Did he spit because of my name, or because he's sick? "Lay off it, Marius. I don't know if I want our Robin associating with royalty. Who's to say we can trust this man to do what's right for our motley crew?"

Wait a minute, do they not know who Rowena's mother was? Who her parents were?

William sighs besides me, distracting me from my thoughts as he whispers, "That's Will Stutley. He goes by Stue. He hasn't stopped sneezing since the flowers started blossoming. Pretty sure he's sneezed out most of his brains in the past two weeks and all that's left is his *sparkling* personality."

Stue groans, pushing a lock of unruly hair out of his face. "I can hear you, Red. As if you wouldn't be a grump if you couldn't stop sneezing and had a constant red nose that scared off the ladies."

"What ladies?" the man next to Stue teases. It's the cook, and though it looked as if he wasn't paying attention a moment before, his intense gaze studies me. His short hair gives his high cheekbones a stark look, making his expression severe. "Don't let them fool you. Stue and Red think all the ladies are in love with them, but it's really Little John who steals all the hearts with his grumpy, grizzly-bear attitude. I'm Dale, by the way. I'm the cook for the camp. Don't complain if you don't like it. I'm a better cook than the rest of the men combined."

Dale's pride puffs out his chest, and I can't help the small smile that makes its way onto my lips as I nod. "I have no complaints. The evening meal was delicious."

Dale nods before leaning forward on his knees, staring into the fire and avoiding conversation, his serious eyes focused on the dancing flames.

The last man yawns; he made it through a few matches tonight, though I noticed he wasn't one for speed. His mussed curly brown hair flops in his eyes as his head dips forward.

William leans toward me again. "That's Much. His magic is in growing plants, but when he uses it, he gets sleepy. He's been working with the seedlings this past week and can barely keep his eyes open."

Everyone goes quiet then, conversations halted as Marius strums his lute to the sounds of the crackling fire and crickets in the forest. There's a pull in my chest, a nagging that won't let me sit in this moment of peace comfortably. Everything is wrapped up inside of me like a tangled mess of colored yarn with knots of feelings tied throughout the threads. I try to pick at one to untangle it but am soon distracted by others, the mess so entwined I can't even define what I'm feeling.

I stare into the orange flames and pick at the internal red-hot string that's wrapped itself tightly around my chest. It pulls itself tighter as I try to decipher its purpose. My breathing quickens as my head flits from each memory of my father lecturing and monologuing the court.

How did I get cursed? I don't remember any specific moment. He never said 'be ye cursed,' so how did it happen?

I tap my fingers against my knee, hazy memories of words my father has spoken, words I can't remember.

Words.

Every time I spoke to my father, he spread the darkness, and I came away not caring about anything and anyone. What did I even do during that time? What have I done in the past five years? Mindlessly read books? Practiced sword fighting with the guards? Did I do anything of substance?

No.

Because my father turned me into a useless puppet.

The only time I've felt my mind clear in the past five years around my father was last night when I looked into Rowena's eyes.

Her magic cured me—at least for the time being.

I wouldn't have needed curing if my father hadn't cursed me or our kingdom to begin with.

I look around the fire pit, taking note of each man's weary expressions. Each one has done something to anger my father like I did.

I need to know. I need to fix this.

"Why?" The word rips from my throat. "Why did my father want each of you dead?"

William barks out a harsh laugh from beside me. "I dared to question why he was raising the taxes at a council meeting when I attended for my father. Father was ill, and I was tired of him doing nothing over the king's ridiculous demands for taxes, so I said something. Next thing I knew, Robin was at my door saying the king wanted me to go on a hunt for the next feast."

We fall silent until Marius chuckles. "I sang a ballad about Solwain and his gift of magic at a banquet." He shakes his head. "I didn't realize your father's hatred of magic ran so deep. Though I can't complain about being rescued by Robin. I much prefer singing out here in the woods now. The audience is more rewarding."

Dale doesn't move his gaze from the fire, but his shoulders stiffen. "You might not remember me, Your Highness, but I worked in the kitchen as Cook's assistant. I dared to offer the king a magical remedy to his sickness last year. My magic influences the properties of food and thus the person who eats it." He shakes his head. "He threw the cup against the wall, screaming at me as if magic were outlawed. He was so enraged. Robin found me the next morning and brought me safely here."

Stue sneezes and wipes his nose on his shirt sleeve again. "I flirted with your father's mistress. Didn't realize it was a crime. Didn't realize your father had his eye on her. It didn't matter that I'm the son of a duke. I got invited to go on a hunt the next day and ended up here." He glares at me. "Would be nice to see my family again, Your Highness. But we can't risk letting our families know we live. Though I'm sure my father would spare some thicker blankets or even a cow to the cause if he knew I was here in the forest."

I stare at Stue, imagining his unruly hair tamed, and him wearing a double-breasted suit to a state event. That's when I recognize him. He must be a bit younger than me, though, because I don't remember growing up with him or training with him during my teenage years.

His words about my father having a mistress stir up another set of feelings I am not up to addressing at the moment.

Much startles, almost making me jump as he throws his head up and looks at me. "I was making too much money with my plant magic. The nobles were hiring me to work in their greenhouses and in their fields. I was hired to help your father's gardeners. When I went to collect my wages, he refused to pay me. So I refused to do more work. He said it was a privilege to help the king. I said privilege wouldn't feed an empty stomach." Much shakes his head, his hand rubbing against his belly as his eyelids droop. "Pretty sure I almost died right there on the castle steps. Instead, Robin showed up, gripping my elbow and walking me away as if she knew what the king ordered without him needing to say a word."

William nods next to me. "I don't know what we'd do without Robin."

Little John grunts but doesn't say anything. I know who he is, though; his face matches one I often saw around the castle and among the guards.

As the flames grow smaller in the pit, the red-hot fire within me burns, fueling a deep-seated fury within me. The man I've looked up to, grown up idolizing and wanting to be like has done all of this? He's ordered the death of good men, and for what? Pride and greed? He's spent his days in debauchery while the rest of us have been cursed by darkness.

The fire burns so intensely within me that I can't sit still. Energy courses through me and I stand, hands fisted at my side. "I'm taking my father down. He's hurt too many to continue to sit on his throne."

Their heads lift, weary eyes meeting mine.

I extend my hand. "Will you help me?"

I look down at William. My cousin, one of my only friends whom I lost—*stolen* from me by my father. There's a crooked grin on his lips, and he nods.

My gaze travels to Little John who grunts, but nods his head. Marius grins, Stue grumbles but agrees, Dale pierces me with a stony gaze, and Much nods his head before dropping it into his hands again.

I clear my throat, the sudden ball of emotion in the way of the words I need to speak. "I don't have siblings, nor many friends. But you are my brothers in misfortune. We've been dealt a terrible hand, and I won't stand for it. May I call you my friends? My comrades in arms?"

"Aye," Marius says, a wicked smile across his face. "But know that Robin leads us. We are *her* band of merry men. Are you willing to join *us*? To submit to *her* leadership?"

Her face, the dusting of freckles across her nose, those brown eyes with flecks of green, and the sassy smile always on her lips come to my mind. I fist my hand, pounding it against my chest over my heart—the sign of respect and dedication among the knights of Lyriva.

"Always."

Marius nods. "Then welcome to the Camp of Robin Hood and her band of"—he pauses looking at each of us—"seven merry men."

Chapter Nine

A Cook Most Astute

Rowena

My magic unfurls through the forest, marking where each animal is. From the squirrels in trees to the rabbits in burrows, I can sense them all. It used to be overwhelming, but through years spent in the forest, I've refined my ability to choose when I sense someone.

A fleeting thought, a long-gone wish to attend the Academy of Radiance, to refine my knowledge and abilities, sneaks into my mind. It's too late now, and I'm in too deep with my plans to dispose of King Ferdinand.

There's a light rustle behind me. Red's heartbeat registers in my magical senses.

"Red, what are you doing?" I hiss. My eyes stay fixed on the trail ahead of me. There's a group of deer beyond the thicket, and if we stay quiet enough, I'll be able to sneak up on the doe who injured her leg recently.

Red's voice is low, barely a whisper. "Now that Alvor is in the camp, I fear for you, Robin. There's no one left to contest the king's claim to the throne."

I huff. "It's a good thing I'm not assassinating anyone today then, isn't it?"

Red growls. "I never liked that plan in the first place, Robin. It'd have stained your soul, and you know it."

"I'd rather have a stained soul and save our people than continue to live in squalor as children suffer."

"So would I," Red says as he steps up behind me. His hand grips my elbow, gently turning me toward him. "Robin, we need to make a real plan, not something half-baked. We can't rely on an unreliable poison."

I shove his hand off my arm. "What do you think I'm trying to do here, Red? I am trying to make a plan, but if I want to avoid notice, then I also need to do my job. Cook needs a whole deer today. Are you going to keep standing here talking and scaring off the herd? Or are you going to go do something productive?"

Red runs his hands through his red curls, puffing them out further from his head. "I just worry about you, Robin. Alvor is here now, and I know the two of you were close—"

"Were close, Red. We were, in the *past*. I have no feelings tied to that man other than the desire to get rid of the rest of his curse and put him on a throne. Now will you leave and get back to camp to go do something other than scare off the game?"

He backs up, his hands in the air. "Robin, you know you're like one of my sisters. I'm just trying to look out for you."

I lift my hand in the air, gesturing from my head to my toes. "What part of this outfit says I need looking out for? My bow and arrow? My hidden knives? The hunting leathers strapped to my body? Go save your protective instincts for a young maiden who actually wants them."

Red smirks, shaking his head, but then melts back into the forest.

A red fox pokes its nose out of its burrow under a tree, and we make eye contact. "Was that too harsh?"

The fox tilts its head, and I shake mine. "What am I doing talking to a fox?"

I close my eyes, letting my magic warm me as it maps out the forest with the glowing presences of the animals. The deer have moved—not unexpected considering the noise Red and I made—and luckily for me, they're closer to the castle now.

I pinpoint the pulsing light, the pain of the doe with the hurt leg calling to me. It's one of the only ways I can stomach my job, knowing I'm giving much-needed relief to a suffering creature, so they can go frolic in animal paradise, or wherever their spirits go.

My boots slip through the undergrowth, and I creep up on the herd. I pull an arrow from my quiver, notching it, holding it at the ready as I maneuver into a clear spot with a perfect line of sight of the doe.

I pull back, the motion second nature as I aim.

I blow out a breath of air as I release the arrow. It hits its mark.

The herd scatters, except for my prey.

I take a moment to observe the light flowing away from the precious animal.

Red was right. I'm not a killer by nature—definitely not an assassin. But the protectiveness inside me is dying to do something. I'm tired of thin stew in camp, of the quiet despair in the castle, and the dwindling joy and happiness in the villages.

So many have died, and I need to do something.

I make quick work of the doe, prepping it to carry to the castle. My mind mulls over ideas of things I can do now—today—to assuage the gnawing need to do something.

The walk through the woods is silent, my noise scaring away the birds and other creatures from my path. I can see their lights flittering away in my mind's eye, as if I'm a creature of death stalking them.

That's what I was going to become yesterday ... maybe it was a good thing King Ferdinand demanded Alvor's death; it saved me from becoming my worst nightmare.

I step out of the forest, and the guards at the side gate straighten. Neither offer to help me carry the doe on my shoulders. Their noses wrinkle, disgust written across their faces as I pass them.

I weave through the vegetable garden until I get to the meat shed. I hang the doe and then go retrieve the two kitchen boys. I pull down the deer I shot two days ago, and together the three of us work to process the meat. We make quick work, and I leave them to clean up the mess as I carry the best cuts to the kitchen for Cook.

I drop a slab of meat on Cook's meat table. She gestures to the bucket in the corner, and I walk over, rinsing off as best as I can. The iron scent stings my nose, and only when I splash my face do I realize there was a streak of blood across it. Cook throws me a ragged towel, and I scrub my face, hands, and arms as best I can.

"This was a good one," Cook says, indicating the meat.

I shrug. My heart still aches over the kill. My stomach churns. I inherited this job from my father and my magic from my mother, but how it's turned into the perfect way to plan a rebellion seems more miracle than happenstance. I'm grateful for it, as it has kept me nimble, out of the way, and able to have a pulse on everything going on in the kingdom as I travel through Sherwood Forest to the villages, a few of which I need to visit soon.

"Yes," I manage to say. "Deer lasts longer than pheasant, and I have ... things to do."

Cook nods, her tight bun and apron immaculate despite being in the kitchen for hours already today. Her eyes widen as her voice drops to a whisper. "Rumor has it there's a duke, favored of the king, traveling to Rovia today. He has a daughter he wants to marry off to their prince. He's taking her dowry with him."

It's a good thing I've got Cook on my side. I swear she's the only sane person in the castle besides myself. I would not be surprised if she has magic but keeps it under wraps. Especially considering Dale was her assistant, the woman must be familiar with magic. That will remain a mystery, as does her name and her secret to apple turnovers. I have plenty of my own secrets; I'll let the woman keep hers.

I wring out my hands, drying them as I look over her counter. "Got any spare rolls for the road? Gonna be a long night hunting."

Cook smirks. "Got some sweet rolls and an extra little something for your newest hunter."

Ah yes. My newest hunter whom my merry men embraced easily as if he was always a part of our crew. I still don't know how I feel about it. I swing between happiness and annoyance, and maybe I'll just accept the fact I can feel both simultaneously.

I'm still mad he took my seat at breakfast this morning. I have *my* spot. He should have instinctively known the head of the table is my spot.

Ridiculous princeling.

Cook moves to another table, and I wave my hands through the air, not wanting to touch my bloodstained clothes. The kitchen is quiet, only short conversations interrupting the silence between all the bustling humans. I close my eyes and let my magic flow. Though every person in the room has a light within them, it's as if they're dimmed, overshadowed by darkness.

This is the king's doing. The unnatural silence—it's because of him.

My nails dig into my palms, and it's only when Cook steps in front of me, a pouch of food in hand, that I shove my feelings back down. I tie the pouch to my belt and look around the kitchen, noting how isolated we are in this corner. "Any suggestions for who needs a dowry?"

Cook tilts her head. "Why don't you let your newest recruit decide?"

I fold my arms, glaring at the infuriating woman. "I'm in charge, not him. I'll decide. Just wanted to know if there was a need I should know about."

Cook arches an eyebrow. "You know exactly what needs to happen, huntress. Teach your new recruit everything. He's the hope for our future, and don't you forget it."

She flips around and doesn't say another word as I slink out the door.

Chapter Ten

A Child Most Hungry

Alvor

I'm a useless prince.

Nobody else was going to say it, but I will.

I can fight with a sword, but I don't know how to chop wood. I can give you a report on all the kingdoms of Miraveil, but ask me what plants I can eat from a forest, and you might as well be asking to die from food poisoning. I have muscles, developed from training with the guards, and where does it land me? Collecting wood for the fire.

That is, if I can even remember how to get back to camp from here.

My boots snap another twig, yet I can't hear sounds; it's so silent in here. A branch from the log I'm carrying jabs me in the side as I twist around, trying to see past the wide trees back to the small clearings Rowena and her men have made for her people. Scratch that—our people.

I need to take responsibility for the mess my father has made. But the longer I've been away from Rowena, the less clear my thoughts seem to be.

Is it the ridiculous curse? Or am I just clueless?

I spot another branch on the ground that looks dry. I pick it up, only to find bright green leaves on its end.

Nope. Not what they asked me to get.

A branch snaps behind me, and I turn to find a woman emerging from behind a tree, two young children clinging to her skirt.

How did they sneak up on me?

I'm useless.

"Hello." My voice comes out scratchy, and I clear my throat before trying again. "Hello, can I help you?"

The woman hesitates before taking a step closer. She bites her lip, looking past me before meeting my gaze. "Do you know where we can find Robin Hood?"

I frown. "Is something wrong?"

There's a sniffling sound, and I look down at the little girl, who buries her face in the woman's skirt. The woman—their mother, maybe?—strokes the young girl's hair. "We heard we could find Robin Hood, and that there'd be safety with his men."

My stomach churns. "Yes. You're quite right."

I turn away, but not before seeing the haunted look in the little girl's gaunt face. The sour taste in my mouth grows more bitter as I lead us through the forest.

A weight lifts off my shoulders when, after passing a few more trees, I can hear Marius's lute. My steps quicken. "This way," I murmur over my shoulder.

The mother's face brightens, hope springing to her eyes.

The trees thin, and I lead them into the clearing near the cook fire. Dale's stirring a pot, and Marius sits on one of the dining logs. Their eyes move quickly from me to the guests trailing behind me.

Marius springs up as if he's a young man, not twenty years my senior. He smiles wide and stops in front of the mother and her children. He strums a happy sound on his instrument as he kneels in the dirt.

"Why hello, weary travelers. Have you come to join us for our midday meal? We're always happy to feed more brave souls like you."

The little girl peeks out from behind her mother while the little boy steps forward, fingers outstretched toward the instrument. Marius moves it forward, offering it to the boy who happily plucks a note on the string before giggling. The mother's shoulders shake, her hand coming up to cover her mouth, as tears streak down her cheeks.

Marius looks up at her and stretches out his hand. She clasps it tightly as she cries. "Thank you. He hasn't laughed in weeks."

Marius grins, but I don't miss the sadness in his eyes. "Well now, you're in the camp of Robin Hood. There is merriment to be had, my young friends! Come sit yourselves down, and we'll feed you a meal."

The little boy grins, his front tooth missing. "Food?"

Marius ruffles his dirty hair. "Why yes, young man. There is plenty of food for you, your sister, and your mother." He winks before stepping back and turning to me. His voice drops to a whisper. "Help Dale, please. I'll entertain them."

I nod and walk over, dropping the wood I collected in the burn pile. Dale points me in the direction of the bowls and spoons, and I grab the deepest ones I can find. When I make it back to the stew pot, I catch sight of a wisp of light traveling from Dale's fingers into the food. He's blocked the young family from seeing his motions, but I'm fascinated as light sprinkles down onto the stew, sinking into the liquid.

Dale looks up, gesturing me over without a word.

"What does your magic do to the food?" I whisper.

"For them? It'll help them stomach it and keep it down. I doubt they've had a good meal in weeks. They're malnourished, so I strengthened the properties of some of the vegetables. Hopefully, it'll speed their recovery." He frowns. "Those children are too skinny."

I nod and deliver two full bowls to the children, before delivering a third to their mother.

Tears stream down her face, twisting my heart.

The woman turns to Marius. "Thank you. We haven't had more than the plants I've been able to scavenge in a week. When I saw the tax collectors this morning, I knew we had to run." Her shoulders shake as emotions overcome her.

Marius places his hand on her shoulder. "You're safe here, ma'am. No more worries, at least for today. Eat up—it's the best stew in the kingdom. While you eat, I'll play a happy song for you and your children."

The minstrel's fingers begin a playful ballad about a merry princess that has smiles growing on everyone's face. It's one I enjoyed hearing myself when I was younger.

How long has it been since I felt like my younger self? Besides those fleeting moments with Rowena that stir up dormant feelings of attraction?

This darkness festering in me, this constant self-deprecation . . . is it really me? Or is it the work of my father?

I move back to Dale's side, and we work in tandem, filling bowls as people trickle in from around camp, welcoming the newcomers and graciously thanking Dale for the single bowl of watery stew they each receive.

Yet, the people smile. Their faces are worn, there's a heaviness weighing down their shoulders, but they don't hesitate to smile and join in singing with Marius.

William makes his way through the line, and when he gets his bowl, I grab one too, following him to a makeshift table placed on the outskirts of the group.

"William, I need your help," I whisper, as we sit, bowls in hand.

He shakes his head. "It's Red, cousin."

I sigh. "Sorry. Red, I could use your help."

"What?" he asks around a mouthful of stew.

"Do you have a map of the kingdom? I want to know which villages have been hit the worst by the taxes."

"Nottingham," he mumbles as he slurps a bite. "Nottingham is the worst. Their sheriff is pure evil and acts as the tax collector. Except he's purposefully collecting more, even though your father has already raised the amount too high as is." He tilts his chin toward the mother and children. "I'd bet they hail from there."

I shrug. "I don't know. I was gathering firewood when they found me in the woods. Somehow I made it back here."

William chuckles. "Any clue where that was?"

I point over my shoulder.

He chuckles. "Okay, so you were in the north forest. Definitely from Nottingham."

"How can you even tell directions in here?"

His face sobers. "When you've been living in the forest for three years, you learn."

William's words are a knife to my heart. "I'm sorry."

William shrugs. "At least I'm not dead."

"Yes, but you've been living in the woods for three years. You're the son of a duke, the king's own nephew."

William arches an eyebrow. "And you're the crown prince. Whatcha gonna do about it?"

I stare down into my bowl, stirring the mysterious contents with my spoon. I take a bite, surprised at the strength of the herbs flavoring the broth and the richness of the meat. Dale's magic at play, no doubt.

My eyes are drawn back to the young mother's. Her clothes are threadbare, the children's no better than rags.

"Whatever it takes, Red. Whatever it takes."

He nods and stands. "Come on. Let me show you our makeshift war room."

Chapter Eleven

A Plan Most Changed

Rowena

I tug my hood over my head, ensuring my cloak hides most of my figure as I stalk into camp. I'm not here as often as I'd like to be, and I've done a decent job of hiding my gender from the recent refugees.

I skirt around the eating area, heading toward our supply area where I'll usually find Little John sharpening a weapon.

I stop in my tracks when I turn the corner and find most of my merry men and Alvor in our makeshift war room. It's nothing more than a large stump next to the weapons shed, where I also keep the map I stole from the library two years ago. I'm only frozen for a second before gathering my wits.

Well, if they thought they could make plans without me, they're wrong. I'm in charge.

I throw the sack of food at Red, who catches it effortlessly as I approach the group.

My hands are on my hips, feet wide as I step up into the last open space in the circle. I stare down at the map, tracing the roads from here to Rovia with my gaze. "Change of plans, men." I look up in time to see Red pull out an apple turnover from the bag. "Red, that's for the princeling over there, a present from Cook."

He grumbles but hands over the baked good to Alvor before passing out the rolls in the bag to the rest of us.

"What's the new plan, Robin?" John asks as he folds his arms. His stoic expression hides how much of a softy he is, but I'm grateful he still recognizes my leadership role.

"We're robbing the rich to feed the poor. Duke Wessex is on his way to barter his daughter's hand to the prince of Rovia. I don't think that should happen, nor does the illustrious duke get to keep his money. He's one of King Ferdinand's closest advisors and has kept more coin than any other noble. It's about time to give it back to those who earned him the coins in the first place."

Red throws me a roll, and I inhale its sweet smell as I rip a piece off with my teeth. The bread practically melts in my mouth, the hint of honey flavoring the wheat flour.

Little John grunts. "Standard plan, then?"

I tilt my head, slowly chewing my roll.

My eyes are drawn to Alvor.

Wild boars, Cook was right! I can't just have the princeling hang around. I need him to see what we're doing and why.

"Nope." I shake my head. "Our princeling needs a change of clothes. He's coming with us. He'll partner with Red."

"Weren't we going to go see my uncle today?" Red speaks around a mouthful of bread.

I shrug. "It'll have to wait. This money isn't waiting, and there are mouths to feed."

Alvor nods, a frown tugging his lips down. "The tax collectors were out this morning."

My lips mirror his. "That means we can expect a family or two to make their way to us today."

"There's already one here," Dale informs me.

My heart sinks. We don't have much more room to expand if we want to keep our camp quiet. No one from the castle knows the forest like I do, and we've miraculously avoided being found by the few men King Ferdinand has sent out into the forest after one of my raids.

But we can't hide forever.

I study Alvor's pensive expression as he stares at the map of Lyriva. I need to get him on the throne soon, but maybe he can learn some things for himself before then.

Marius strums his lute. "Are we all to be bandits today, Robin?"

I nod. "Yes."

Red's mouth twists down. "I don't want to play babysitter, Robin. Alvor doesn't even know the woods."

There's a grunt from Red, and I catch a quick glimpse of Alvor's elbow moving away from his ribs. I hold in my chuckle and step away from the table, settling onto a chopped log so I can rest my feet for a moment. "It's not like he's useless, Red. Alvor knows how to use a sword, and if I remember right, he's decent with a bow."

Alvor bristles. "*He* is right here, thank you very much. I'm good with a sword. My shooting skills have improved since the last time we tested them, though only marginally. I'm very good at staying out of the way, so tell me what to do and I'll do it." He folds his arms, glaring daggers at his cousin.

I tap my chin playfully, eyeing up the group of men before me. Little John shakes his head and stalks away as Marius begins a lively tune, his eyes drinking in the small dramatic scene before him.

Can't deny my minstrel of ballad fodder now, can I?

"I still don't want to leave you running around without a buddy, princeling," I say. "You might accidentally get in the way."

Alvor folds his arms, eyes narrowing as he turns to face me fully. "I'm not useless."

I stand back up and fold my arms, stepping in front of him. "Good. Glad you know that. Ready to prove it?"

"Bring it on." He leans forward, his face getting dangerously close to mine as his voice drops to a lower timbre. "Rowena."

A shiver travels up my spine with the whisper of my name. It's a deliciously foreboding sensation.

This is *definitely* a bad idea.

Chapter Twelve

A Bandit Most Beautiful

Alvor

I walk out from William's hut—I mean, Red's hut. That's going to take some getting used to. I'm still in my cream-colored shirt from when I left the castle, but my pants have been traded out for green linens. The brown leather vest is snug around my chest, seeing as I'm a tad broader than Red, but the rest fits me well. Including the knee-high leather boots.

All I'm missing is a hood. I walk out to our motley crew, all of us matching in our attire, except for Rowena. Her jerkin is green, along with her shoulder guards, her sleeves a cream color, and her pants a dark brown. Her hood and cloak, a similar dark green color to her jerkin, hide her braid. When she pulls it in front of her, clasping it over her chest, her entire figure is hidden.

Ah, so that's how she hides her gender and identity. Not that anyone seems to think of her as more than a huntress. The disguise is effective, unless you know her well. But nobody seems to know the Rowena I grew up with, just the persona of Robin Hood standing before me.

Granted, the rumors of banditry I vaguely remember never mentioned a female leader. It was always a group of men—hooded, hidden, and fiercely threatening.

Yup. That's our group. Fiercely threatening.

I don't really want to go rob Duke Wessex. He's been kind to me. But I also know he's in my father's pocket. The idea of delivering his coins to my countrymen in need has an appeal to it that shoves my doubts out of my mind. I'm already an outlaw, and Marius has dubbed me the Outlaw Prince, so I might as well run with it. Though it's not as easy to shed the desire to follow the laws. But there's a small fire burning in my chest—a warmth I haven't felt in a long time urging me to push past the laziness I've become accustomed to under my father's curse.

Rowena clears her throat, the quiet conversations dying as she draws our attention. We gather around her, everyone naturally turning toward her for instructions. "Duke Wessex is heading toward Rovia. We'll cut him off when he passes through the north portion of the forest. I want Stue and Much to drop from the trees in front to startle the group. Little John and Marius will flank them. I'll walk out, while Red and Princeling will watch the sides."

I raise my hand. "Can I have a different nickname, please?"

Rowena arches her eyebrow as she smirks. "Do you have a better one in mind?"

I shrug. "Well, no. I just don't like that one."

Her eyebrows raise. "Then, no. As soon as you, or someone else, comes up with one that rolls off the tongue just as well, you'll be Princeling, and that's that."

"Look, Rowena—"

She straightens as her eyes narrow. "Robin."

I sigh. "Fine. Robin. Wouldn't it be better to use something less conspicuous? Something that won't give my identity away? Isn't that why you want me to call you *Robin*?"

Her nose wrinkles, and I have the oddest desire to bop it with my finger. *Excuse me, brain? What in the world are you thinking? Absolutely not.*

I fold my arms, just so I can make sure to keep my hands to myself.

"You've convinced me, princeling. But to throw everyone off your case, I'm going to call you something equally absurd. I dub thee Sir Snow White, for your complexion and need for all things to be right and proper."

Snickers erupt from the men, the teasing and ribbing commencing immediately. My cheeks heat and I glare at Rowena, which only makes her smile wider. "What? Is that not a distraction from who you are? I'll be in the heat of the heist and call out for Sir Snow White, and everyone will be so distracted by the name that they won't think to see the big strong man coming at them with his sword. It's perfect." She props her hands on her hips, tilting her chin up and smiling wide.

Feelings long suppressed resurrect from where I've buried them deep within me. With one look, she's excavated them, set them on fire, and reminded me why I was half in love with her as a young teenager.

I want to draw her into my arms and kiss her until she's smiling with me instead of at me. I want to knock her hood off her head, twine my fingers into her hair, and hold her against me, blocking out the darkness of the world as my lips dance with hers.

Except we can't.

More like, I won't.

Because Rowena is the leader of a band of outlaws, the savior of those less fortunate, and the charitable heart that has kept my kingdom afloat while I've been convalescing under a dark enchantment, letting my father ruin my kingdom.

Her dislike of me is palpable and depressing.

The high of momentary desire is brought low by my dark reality. Rowena will never care for me as I've cared for her. She may have saved my life, a testament to her kindness, but that doesn't mean her heart is anywhere close to reciprocating my admiration.

I run a hand over my jaw, pulling myself together as I stare at the woman who has long haunted my heart. "Fine. It'll be a good laugh, I'm sure."

Little John's chest stops rumbling, the only sign of his merriment. "Let's go, men. Off to spread the wealth."

Everyone breaks into a jog, Robin at the head, leading us down a deer trail northbound. We're quiet, the only noise our labored breathing, until Marius breaks into song. There are groans from everyone, yet no one stops him from singing.

There once was a band of bandits
Led by a Robin fair
Who fought to bring the kingdom
Coins of gold so rare

It was a merry band of seven
Who were the needed spark
They fought against the oppression
Of a king who spread the dark

The band was led by Robin Hood
With his giant friend Little John
Then came along Much the Miller
Who only stopped to yawn

Next came William
Though Scarlett was his name
He soon became Red
Because of his fiery mane

They were ever a-smiling
Once Marius joined the throng

For even Dale the Cook
Could not resist the song

On days when Stue was a-sneezing
They ever began to say
That Robin chose a good one
Who sneezed all their struggles away

The last to join the crew
Could not be kept away
For Snow White was the name
Of the royal who got away

Snow White left the great big castle
To join our motley crew
And now we seven men go dancing
To steal coins as we do

For the Royal and our Robin
Shall lead us to the day
When the evil king shall be deposed
And light shall guide the way.

A quiet cheer escapes the lips of a few of the men, emboldened by Marius's witty lyrics. But I bite my tongue and watch Rowena's back, hoping to catch a glimpse of her reaction.

She looks back briefly, a wry smile on her face. "I've heard better Marius. This one is going to make people speculate, you know."

I snort. "As if they don't already."

Rowena spins around, sidestepping William, who is between us, until she's looking up into my face. "Listen, people don't know who I am. Let's keep it that way."

"And let's keep going," Little John pipes up from behind me. "We don't have time for squabbles."

Rowena huffs, her cheeks tinted red, emphasizing the dusting of freckles across the bridge of her nose that I'm starting to adore. She glares at me before spinning back around, pulling her hood and cloak tighter around her as she moves back to the front of our line.

Everyone goes quiet as we race through the underbrush. My mind feels lighter after staring into Rowena's eyes. I'm more determined to prove I'm ready to make the changes this kingdom needs—that she needs.

And maybe, just maybe, one day I'll be able to rid myself of the lingering darkness in my mind.

Chapter Thirteen
A Lady Most Fiery

Rowena

I hold up my hand, and my men and Alvor still behind me. I look back at Little John and nod. He grabs Alvor's shoulder and steers him through the underbrush to the spot he'll lie in wait. Red takes up his post just ahead of Alvor.

We all pull out the cloth masks from our bags and tie them securely around our faces. The rest of the men lift their hoods, their faces hidden in the shadows.

My gaze roves over everyone, inspecting their disguises. When we rob a noble, I'm extra careful to make sure Red and I can't be recognized. Now I have to worry about Alvor too. Alvor, who really should not look this handsome as a bandit—it's a crime against banditry.

I drag my eyes away to see Marius smirking at me.

Ugh, ridiculous minstrel. That ballad he made up got to me. Long-dead daydreams of a future with a certain princeling flash through my mind. But I push them away; there's no time to think about it now.

I sneak across the road and climb a tree with a thick branch that hangs low over the road. I stay close to the trunk, waiting for the signal Little John will give when he sees the carriage approaching.

Time passes slowly before a whistle cuts through the silence. I slow my breathing, listening for the sounds of a carriage as I wiggle out on my branch and precariously perch myself over the road. I hear the clomp of the horse hooves first, followed by a squeaky wheel and jangle of harnesses. There aren't many other sounds, which is in our favor. One carriage is easy to handle.

I study the carriage as it approaches. Duke Wessex is traveling light today. I'm sure being in the king's pocket gives him a sense of security others lack. The assumption is not wrong, seeing as this will be our first time robbing him. A wave of excitement flows through me as I picture the pleasure it will be to see him in the king's castle after robbing him, knowing exactly where each of his greedy coins went.

It's one of the joys of banditry—when I go back to the castle, I can watch the nobles squirm as they spread rumors and try to hide just how much money they lost to a small group of bandits. They never know that the huntress hiding in the shadows was the one to threaten them—and I'm going to keep it that way.

A whistled trill reaches my ears, and Much and Stue slip from the foliage blocking the carriage's path. Their bows are notched with arrows aimed at the guard sitting atop the carriage. I don't see them—nor do I hear them—but I know Marius and Little John have flanked the travelers.

The guards rein in the horses, who shake their heads, hooves shifting nervously across the dirt at the threats standing before them.

It's my turn.

I grip the branch beneath my feet before swinging my legs down, dropping to the ground in a crouch. I wait a moment, making sure my cloak has settled and my mask hasn't moved, before dramatically rising.

What's banditry without drama?

Boring.

The door to the carriage swings open, a potbellied man descending from the steps. "Excuse me. What is going on here? Do you not know who you have stopped?" Duke Wessex says as he waddles in our direction. Duke Wessex is not a man accustomed to exercise, and his huffing and puffing is quite entertaining. He gives the horses a wide berth as he walks right up to Stue.

Stue, good man that he is, lowers his bow, just enough that the arrow points at the duke's foot.

We're not killers. It's something we agreed on from day one.

One of his guards jumps down from the top of the carriage. "Your Grace, please back away from the bandits."

At least someone has a good head on their shoulders.

I step in front of Stue, forcing Duke Wessex to move backward. I guess I can grace him with a few answers to his questions.

I drop my voice low, something I've practiced for four years and still find entertaining. I channel my father's no-nonsense tone. "Duke Wessex, we have come for your coins."

He wipes a hand across his forehead, shaking his head as his cheeks grow even more rosy. "You shall not have them. All I have in my carriage is my daughter's dowry."

I nod. "That is what we are after."

The duke splutters. "You cannot. She is off to marry the prince of Rovia. You would dare endanger such a beneficial political alliance for our kingdom?" He sticks his nose high in the air until he realizes he can't see me when he does that. He drops his chin again, ruining the noble air he was attempting to pull off.

I spread my arms out to my side, gesturing at the two men behind me. "Then your daughter is welcome to marry one of my merry men, for today we are taking her dowry. You may relinquish it quietly and with ease, or we may tie you up and force you to hand over the dowry."

The duke turns to his guard. "Captain. You must tell them to stop this! At once!"

The poor guard looks around, noting that he's outnumbered. "Your Grace, it would be better if we did not fight. I only brought one other guard, and your daughter is in the carriage, frightened."

Duke Wessex's lips flap, as do his arms, as he turns from side to side. Red steps out from the foliage, next to the door of the carriage with Little John behind him. "But . . . but . . . the dowry! The marriage! She's going to be a princess!"

The carriage door slams open once more. A petite young woman with a fancy red dress and dark hair steps out. Her cheeks are flushed and face pinched as she stares at the Duke. "I told you I do not want to marry Rovia's prince, Father. But you didn't listen to me. Take this as the sign it is—I will not marry a man I have never met, no matter if it makes me a princess. I'd rather marry one of these bandits, for at least they have honor, unlike you—riding away without telling a soul where I'm going. And for what? So you can avoid the king's suspicions? You don't even care that I'm heartbroken over Prince Alvor. So no, I will not leave Lyriva."

The girl stomps her foot and folds her arms, glaring with the fiery darts of a woman fed up with never being taken seriously. It's a familiar expression, and I can't help myself.

I clap.

I keep clapping, even as the duke turns his enraged face toward me. "What are you doing?"

"Celebrating a woman who knows her mind and who has the guts to speak it. You'd do well to listen to her, for she'll guide you wisely." I walk around Stue until I'm in sight of the young lady. "My lady, if you ever wish to fall in love with a man who will respect your opinions and feelings, I offer you any of my merry men. They would do well to have a woman with such spirit at their side."

The young lady blushes, her hand coming up to her cheeks before brushing away a stray curl that had fallen loose from her updo during her passionate speech. Her eyelashes flutter as if she's suddenly bashful in the face of my praise. "See, Father? These men understand me. So it's either me or the dowry. Give them the money, and I'll go home and choose who I want to marry from the local noblemen. Or keep the money, and I'll run away with these bandits."

You go, girl!

Wait.

WHAT?

I don't want a noblewoman in camp. I have enough ladies in camp making eyes at my men as it is. I don't need someone else to mess up the way things are. I've already got a prince doing that job nicely.

I give her a short bow. "My lady. I'd be happy to send any of my men to marry you at your own home. I'm afraid the woods would be no place for a fine young woman with tender sensibilities."

The girl puts her hands on her hips and scowls at me. "What happened to me knowing my own mind? You know what. Forget it. I choose banditry." She walks to Red and hooks her arm through his. "Come on, bandit. We're leaving."

Red looks at me, his eyes wide, before following, more like being dragged by, the young lady into the forest.

We're all in shock. I mean, I am, and when I look at Duke Wessex, it's confirmed. His face is pale, his hands are shaking as he stares after his daughter, tracking her progress through the forest until we can't hear her chattering voice anymore.

"Welp." I pull out an arrow from the sheath on my back. "That was unexpected. Now, about that dowry."

The duke's face falls, his hands trembling as he waves at his carriage. "Take it. Just take it, and take care of my daughter. Better she be with you than in the hands of the king, anyway."

Not sure what that last line meant, but I'm not going to look a gift horse in the mouth. I gesture to Little John who approaches the carriage and unhooks the treasure box from the back. He nods at me and slinks into the woods.

I turn to the captain. "Thank you for your business, gentleman. We'll be off."

I'm about to step into the forest when the duke calls out, "Wait!"

I turn and Much stops, shadowing me, bow and arrow at the ready.

The duke takes a step toward me before being stopped by his guard. "Promise to take care of her. Promise that she'll come to no harm. And promise that you will not let her return to the king's court until after she's married."

I fist my hand, placing it over my heart before bowing, even as confusion fills me. "On my honor, I promise no harm will befall your daughter. She will be cared for and treated with the respect owed a lady."

He nods, eyes glistening. "Thank you."

I give him another slight bow, a pang in my heart going out to the poor man. It's one thing to lose coins; it's another to watch your child walk away.

We slip into the forest, and I soon lose myself in the leaves and trees. I hang back, not ready to confront the chaos this lady is about to bring.

For some reason, I can't recall her name. I know I've seen her before. It's on the tip of my tongue, but I can't remember it for the life of me.

Footsteps come up behind me. They're Alvor's, and I hate that I know that, but his steps are heavier than the rest of my men who are used to treading lightly as they walk through the woods.

Not Alvor. He's like an elephant from one of the eastern countries.

Maybe I really should give him hunting lessons. He could use a refresher on the art of stealth.

No.

Bad idea.

I don't want him sneaking up on me more than he already is trying to.

"What are you going to do with Maid Marian, Rowena?" His voice is low and quiet.

I huff but keep walking, keeping my gaze trained ahead. "So that's who she is. Just our luck. Though I thought she was called Lady Marian."

He groans. "Technically, she's Lady Marian, but her father always praised her for her beauty and virtue, and began calling her Maid Marian. The moniker stuck. Guess you're not the only one who likes to dole out nicknames."

I feel like growling. But ladies don't growl. "Just because I'm clever doesn't mean other people are."

He chuckles, and I feel betrayed when my insides warm at the sound.

Alvor gently grabs my shoulder, stopping me in my tracks. My other merry men have abandoned me, leaving me alone with this prince who is altogether too tempting for my own good.

His arrestingly blue eyes meet mine. "You are clever, Rowena. More than that, you are kindhearted. But you don't need to carry the weight of everything on your shoulders by yourself. Let me help you."

At some point he pulled off his hood and mask, which allowed a lock of dark brown hair, almost black, to flop across his forehead. My fingers act without my permission, pushing it back into place and gently stroking the side of his forehead before they drop again, burned by the innocent touch.

Our gazes are locked in a battle. For what? No idea. All I know is I won't be the first one to look away; it'd be admitting defeat, or cowering away from whatever is growing between us.

Because there *is* something.

I can feel it as I'm drawn into his embrace and as his face inches closer. His nose brushes against mine, and I can't help it anymore. My eyelids close. My hands come up, pressing against his waist as my heart races. His hands gently grip my elbows, pulling me closer with a slow gentleness that has my stomach fluttering.

A branch snaps behind me, and I suck in a sharp breath. I step back, leaning away from the delectable prince who holds me like I'm fragile.

Not delectable.

Not mine.

Not possible.

He's a prince, and I'm a huntress.

The words run through my mind, brought on by the snap of a branch that could only be Little John. It's his sign, his warning of testing the waters whenever he comes upon me, making sure I know he's there.

Which means he's seen how close I've gotten to Alvor, and just how much I want to throw myself into the prince's arms.

I don't move. I'm frozen, unsure of how to break out of this moment without revealing more than I want to.

Because Alvor is not wrong.

The weight I've been carrying is heavy, and I'm ready to pass it on, or at least share the burden with someone.

Alvor has nice shoulders.

Stop it before he breaks your heart . . . again.

I snap my eyes open . . . and run.

Chapter Fourteen

A Dowry Most Large

Alvor

A branch hits me in the face, but I don't even care, because my heart is currently experiencing acute torture.

Rowena ran away from me. My lips were a breath away from hers, and then she stepped back and ran. I know I wasn't imagining the tension between us. The way she leaned into me and the spark of desire in her eyes told me the feelings between us are not a hallucination.

It was there. It was real.

But then she ran away.

I follow the trail, trusting it'll get me back to camp or that someone will come and find me if I don't return in a reasonable amount of time.

My heart twists again. Absolute torture.

Because I know the second I get back to camp, Lady Marian is going to recognize me. She's sweet and has flirted with me even though I was cursed and uninterested. Though the backbone she showed today doesn't actually surprise me. I think there's a healthy dose of stubbornness underneath the sweetness. My esteem toward her was raised by watching the debacle on the road. But still, there's an arresting set of brown eyes with emerald flecks that enchant me every time I look into them that leave no room for another woman.

Plus, I'm the prince. Who knows if Lady Marian was interested in me because of my title, her father, or whatever other reason might come to a young woman's mind. I just ... don't want this refuge to become like the court. I liked having Rowena all to myself. At least, when she's not running away from me.

Dread pools in my stomach.

Is it a little conceited of me to think she'll cling to me when I get to camp? Yes. Let's call it pride-based caution.

In reality, I'm spiraling.

I break through the last group of trees and enter the clearing around the main eating area. The camp has an interesting setup. Each cluster of tents or huts surrounds a personal firepit. But there's also a large clearing with makeshift tables and stump chairs, with a large pit where Dale cooks. Beyond the clearing is the training grounds, a place I've yet to visit beyond watching some of the men spar, but I am now itching to become acquainted with.

I need something to do with my hands, somewhere to channel the convoluted feelings I don't have time to inspect and name.

"Snow White, come assist me," Little John yells from where he's standing by the merry men's circle of huts. Heads turn our way from the practice grounds and general gathering place, but I ignore them. I focus on the giant of a man who I have a sneaking suspicion broke a branch on purpose to ruin my moment with Rowena.

He's not on my *favorite persons* list right now.

I stalk toward him. "What do you need, Little John?"

He narrows his eyes and hooks his thumbs in his belt. "Come help me sort the dowry. We'll save some for Lady Marian, but we need to deliver the rest to the poor. Robin told me you're to pick where they go. A test of sorts to see if you know your kingdom."

I scoff. "A test she means me to fail? She knows I don't know the needs of my people as I should."

Little John shrugs. "Then you'll have to figure it out, won't you? But you won't with that attitude."

I glare at him—he doesn't even flinch. Wretched curses, he's right. My attitude needs an adjustment. I drop my arms, shoulders sagging. "Yes. I will figure it out."

"Like you'll figure out how to court our Robin right proper like?" Little John drops his voice to a whisper.

I arch an eyebrow. "What does that mean?"

He folds his arms, his jaw clenching as he stares at me for a moment. "I've got two eyes, young prince. I know you fancy our Robin. But you don't deserve her. No one does, so you'll have to earn the right to court her. Show her you'll honor her wishes and goals. Until then, I'll keep breaking branches."

I knew it.

My heart races at his perceived threat, and I take a deep breath, reminding myself I'm not in danger from Little John's words, though they make me feel like fleeing.

He's only spoken the truth.

I'm not who I want to be, and I'm not where I want to be if I were to court Rowena.

Because I *am* going to court her. Courtly rules or not, she's the queen our kingdom needs. She's been a better ruler than my father or I have been in the past five years. She deserves a true crown to prove it, and I want to help her continue to lead with light.

I let out my breath slowly, letting my muscles relax so I don't feel like slugging Little John quite so much when I look back at him. "You're right. I will work to earn her favor. But know I'm not perfect, and neither is she. I will never be good enough, but I will keep trying every day to be worthy of her. That's the best I can promise you."

He nods. "That's all I ask, princeling. Promising any more would mean you weren't right for our Robin."

I arch an eyebrow. "Was that a test?"

He arches his brows. "Of course it was. No man can stand next to our Robin without being able to control his emotions and evaluate his words. You have a healthy amount of pride, but it's balanced well with your humility. You'll make a good king one day, if you can win over our Robin."

My lips twitch. "*Win over* being the key words."

He slaps me on the shoulder, almost knocking me over with his strength. "I believe in you, young prince. Now, let's organize these coins into sacks. Tomorrow we'll spend the morning traveling the forest and delivering them to the villages. No better way to get to know your people than to be among them."

I slap his back, only to have my hand come away stinging. "Wiser words have never been spoken, Little John."

We work quickly, Little John producing a satchel full of scraps of fabric. We put a few coins in each cloth, tying them into small bundles that can easily be slipped under door frames or through open windows. There are enough coins for fifty households, though we save the jewelry for Lady Marian.

We stuff the bundles into two satchels and hide them under Little John's cot in his hut. Our stomachs rumble, and we share a chuckle as we walk toward the eating area just as Dale rings the dinner bell. I send a plea to Solwain that the meal will be uneventful, but at this point, I don't even know if he'll listen.

Chapter Fifteen

A Heart Most Confused

Rowena

The dinner bell rings—Dale's signal to gather and get food while it's still warm.

But I can't walk out there yet.

First of all, I almost kissed a prince.

Second, Lady Marian is out there, and I don't want her to know who I am.

Third, well, do I really need a third reason? Two is enough to make me feel like I'm barely able to breathe.

I peek out of my hut; no one is around. Probably because I chose the one farthest away from everyone for privacy reasons.

Wild boars, I don't need privacy right now; I need someone to help me figure out what is going on in my life.

I hear the strumming of a lute, and my heart picks up. "Marius!"

The sounds stop, replaced by quiet steps as Marius rounds the corner and approaches my hut. "Robin?"

"Yes. I need your help. Get in here."

Marius, true to his good nature, quickly enters my hut without question. He makes himself comfortable on a stool and begins playing a new tune, one I hope doesn't go to the ballad he decided to make earlier.

"Robin, how may I help you?" Marius asks with a calm I only wish I felt.

"What do I do about Lady Marian?"

Marius shrugs. "What do you wish? Most of the people in the camp know you keep to yourself. You can avoid dinner; I can bring you a bowl. Or you can show your face, though you might want to wear a disguise. You could wear your normal cloak and face away from everyone."

He strums his lute as I pace the few feet of space in the enclosure. He stops suddenly. "Robin. What's the real issue here?"

I groan and tug at my braid. "It's the ridiculous princeling. I don't know what to do with him."

Marius plucks a note. "You don't have to do anything with him, Robin. He's a man and perfectly capable of figuring out his life on his own. You are not his mother."

I stop and glare. "That's not what I meant."

Marius waves a hand, a smirk playing on his lips. "Then please, enlighten me."

I tap my foot. "Nothing I say can make it into one of your ballads. Do you understand?"

He smiles. "I'll make a deal with you. I will keep your secrets until your wedding. Then I shall have free game to make all the songs I want."

I roll my eyes. "What wedding?"

Marius shrugs. "I don't know, just whenever you get married. Then I can make all the songs about Robin Hood that I want."

I take a deep breath. "Fine."

Marius chuckles. "Now. Tell me how you really feel about our fair prince."

I flop down onto my cot, lean against the log wall, and stare at the thatched roof. "I'm torn up inside. One minute I hate him, the next I don't. I want to go out there and spend time with him, but I don't want Lady Marian to know who I am. I want to, for one night, feel like a normal woman, but I don't even know what that would be like, Marius. I've been doing this for so long now that I feel like I've lost a part of me. Alvor says the curse stole who he was from him, but I think it's done the same for me, just in a different way. I've become someone I don't want to be."

Marius strums the notes of a common lullaby, the tender sounds soothing. "When was the last time you practiced your magic?"

I shrug. "This morning."

"Focus on it now, Robin. Find the light inside of you and cling to it. That is who you are."

He falls silent, and when he doesn't say anything more, I do as he asked. I close my eyes, diving into the special place I imagine is by my heart, where the light resides. My inner eye opens, the light mapping out everyone around me. The shapes of animals hidden in the brush and trees, and the light flickering in the humans in camp shine bright in my mind.

Except one.

One is barely burning. There's a darkness wrapped around it.

Alvor.

My heart lurches. I want to pull him toward me, as if I could somehow cure him of the darkness trapped within him.

A sharp note brings me back to the present, and I open my eyes to see Marius's sheepish face.

"Sorry," he says. "I didn't mean to break you from the moment."

I wave my hand. "It's fine. That helped, thank you."

He nods. "So will you be joining us at dinner tonight?"

My pulse races. "I want to, but I'll need a disguise."

Marius tilts his head. "When was the last time you wore a dress, Robin? I think that might be just the disguise you need."

I try to remember the last time I wore something even close to a skirt, but nothing comes to mind. "Do you think so?"

Marius nods. "I think a dress would be just the thing, and if you happen to sit next to and flirt with a certain royal, I don't think anyone would balk at it, or even realize who you are, except the merry men." He chuckles. "Even then, some of them might not recognize you if you leave your hair down as well."

An idea grows in my mind, and I hop off my bed, reaching underneath to grab a chest.

Marius stands, letting himself out without a word.

The lid creaks as I open it, its age showing. But the contents inside are just as pristine as they were when I packed them five years ago. I move aside Father's knife belt and sword, and find exactly what I'm looking for.

It's out of fashion, but it should fit me.

I unfold the garment gently, holding it up to myself before flouncing the skirt.

One of my mother's dresses. Not one of her fanciest ones, but the one I remember her wearing often when she'd spend the afternoons with me. The simple cut is beautiful, with a square neckline, pleated waist, and full skirt. The sage-green color always complemented Mother's rosy complexion. I hold it up to my face, breathing in the last traces of her smell.

I no longer can remember if she actually smelled like roses, the scent of which still clings to the dress. It may not be her, but rather the dried roses in the chest. Either way, in this moment, it feels as if I'm surrounded by my mother—a presence I greatly miss.

I quickly change, forcing back the tears of grief threatening to overtake me as I lace up the sides of the dress. I undo my braid, letting my wild curls run free. I leave my boots on, seeing as I don't have another pair, but the dress should hide them for the most part.

I do a test spin, enjoying the movement of the skirt of the dress as I box up my feelings and shove them onto a dusty shelf in my brain.

There's no time for grief tonight.

Tonight is about gathering information from Lady Marian and spending time with Alvor.

The man I ran away from after we almost kissed.

Yep. Nothing can go wrong tonight. It's going to be fine.

Chapter Sixteen

A Stew Most Deadly

Alvor

Little John falls into step with me as we walk to the makeshift kitchen. Dale leans over his large pot, stirring the steaming liquid. The scent of root vegetables and meat greets my nose. Stew again, but because it's Dale's, I'm not complaining. The man makes a simple meal fill the stomach and nourish the soul.

I grab a wooden bowl from the stack on the table and fall into line. My stomach grumbles as the scent of ham wafts toward me. I'm not used to two meals a day, maybe three if we're lucky, and my treacherous body is betraying my secret. But I will not complain. I'm lucky this group is willing to feed me when all my father has done to them is made their lives harder.

A frown pulls at my lips, made deeper when a gasp sounds from behind me.

A girlish giggle has my hackles rising. "Prince Alvor?!"

I turn, pasting on a neutral expression as I face my doom. Lady Marian approaches, her arm still hooked through William's. For as wise as William is, he seems to be besotted with the woman beside him. I hope this conversation doesn't sway his feelings. Maybe today is my lucky day and Lady Marian has moved on from me.

Whispers erupt through the onlookers.

I figured most knew who I was, but now there is no doubt in my mind. My identity is no longer secret, nor will this conversation be private, if Lady Marian has anything to do with it.

I bow in greeting. "Hello, Lady Marian."

Her hand comes up to cover her mouth. "Prince Alvor, I'm so pleased to see you. You know, your father announced you died in a tragic accident. To think you're here in the forest with Robin Hood and his merry men!"

I grimace. "Yes, it's quite a tale."

Lady Marian turns to William, her hand lingering on his arm as she looks up into his face with . . . is that adoration?

"Was dear William involved? Did he help save you from your tragic ending?"

The way she says his name, coupled with the look on her face, takes a weight off my shoulders while reminding me to be humble. Because I'm not the only titled man hiding in the forest. If Marian knows William's name, then she's aware of who he is, too.

But maybe she doesn't know who he is, and is instead smitten with his bandit persona.

Hmm, maybe there is more to Lady Marian than I first thought.

Shame fills me, reminding me not to judge the woman before me, because who knows what she's really like outside of court and my father's influence.

William scratches the back of his neck. "I wasn't there for everything, but he is staying with me while he's here."

Marian beams. "How kind of you, William. Oh, that's right! The two of you are cousins. What a glorious family reunion!"

William's eyes meet mine, and I can't help the rueful smile that grows on my lips. "Glorious, indeed."

Lady Marian turns back to me. "Who else is in this delightful little camp? I've yet to meet your leader officially. Robin Hood, right? He's such a strapping man to lead all of you on your grand adventures."

I pinch my lips between my teeth, reining in my chuckle, and watch with amusement as William's eyes widen.

Time for me to make my exit and let him handle the questions.

I turn back in line, only to find I'm next. Dale scoops a steaming ladle full of stew into my bowl and nods. I whisper my thanks before finding an empty table, hopefully out of eyesight from William and Marian.

I seat myself and take a bite of my food, the creamy potatoes, chunk of ham, and savory herbs reminding me of Cook's meals. A pang of homesickness shoots through my heart. My solitude is interrupted when William and Marian slide into the unoccupied bench on the other side of the table from me. I scan the area, but all the seats are taken, save for the few across from me.

I drop my gaze, focusing on my bowl of food as I hide my disappointment. It's no longer about avoiding Lady Marian. I just would like . . . space.

I take another bite, purposefully avoiding conversation with my tablemates. When I look around again for a means to escape, movement catches my eye.

My heart stops, my spoon falling back into the bowl as I stare at the woman walking toward me.

Rowena is wearing a dress—an article of clothing I haven't seen her wear in years.

Her hair falls down across her shoulders and back in waves, a rich brown with streaks of gold threaded throughout the curly locks. Her face is scrubbed clean, and with the square neckline on her sage-green dress, she looks sweet and feminine. It's a stark contrast to her hunting leathers. She looks so different that I doubt many here would recognize her in this outfit.

But I do.

This is the Rowena of our younger years. Seeing her like this has memories of when the little slip of a girl, with braids flying behind her, would challenge the squires and noblemen to archery matches. Though she's a woman now, I can't help but see the young girl who played chess to pass the time, and often beat any boy or man who took it upon themselves to challenge her to a match. She was a girl who laughed freely and who caught my eye, even at a young, tender age. Rowena cared for others and stood up for any who needed a champion.

Though, she is no young girl now.

No, standing before me is a gorgeous woman.

My heart races, and I take a long breath, exhaling slowly. But it does no good, especially when she stares straight at me.

Her eyes flick to my dinner companions, a frown tugging down on her lips for only a second before she fixes a pleasant expression on her face.

Rowena walks over with all the grace of a titled woman. I stand up as she approaches the table. "Mind if I join you?" she coos, in a tone I swore I'd never hear come out of her mouth. Her coquettish grin shocks me after the verbal barbs we've traded over the past two days.

Lady Marian speaks for me. "Of course! Oh, it's so wonderful to see another lady here in the camp. Please, tell me your name; I've never met you before."

Rowena looks at me, her eyes widening by a fraction. My manners kick in, the years of training coming to my rescue. "Lady Marian, may I introduce Lady Rowena, a family friend. She happened to take leave of court before you were introduced, but she's someone I've admired for many years."

Lady Marian sighs dramatically. "Oh, isn't that so sweet." She gently smacks William's chest. "Don't you see how smitten he is with her? Oh, they're so in love. I do so wish for someone to look at me with such a look of affection one day."

My eyes meet Rowena's, and she smiles wryly before sitting down. I take my seat again, and when William leans over, whispering in Marian's ear, the young woman blushes and giggles.

Rowena coughs, and the conspiratorial look between us does more to fix the hurt from her running away than any of the fake flirtations of a moment ago.

Lady Marian takes a bite of food but doesn't let that stop her from continuing our conversation. "So, Prince Alvor, how long have you been courting Lady Rowena?"

The food in my mouth turns to ash as I try to swallow. It gets stuck in my throat, and as I cough into my shoulder, Rowena pounds on my back. I lean over, sucking in great gulps of air when I catch Rowena's answer.

"Our courtship is very . . . recent."

Chapter Seventeen

A Courtship Most Recent

Rowena

Excuse me, brain? What were those words that just came out of my mouth? What was I thinking?

You know what? I wasn't thinking.

It's something about wearing this ridiculous dress and seeing that look of appreciation in Alvor's eyes that did it to me.

It's all *his* fault.

I hook my arm through his and lean against his shoulder.

Ugh, of course he has nice muscles too. And he smells like pine trees after rain, my favorite smell.

It's not fair, but it's too late to change anything. I've committed.

Slowly, Alvor turns his head to look down at me. I look up into those blue eyes I'm mildly obsessed with—which I will deny until the day I die. His eyebrows are arched, and his lips twitch at the corners. "Fairly recent?"

I widen my eyes, mentally communicating the threat that I will string him up by his toes if he doesn't play along with this scheme. I *have* to protect my identity, and Lady Marian must *not* learn that I'm Robin Hood, so this is what I'm running with—a random out-of-touch noblewoman, and not a huntress bandit.

I know, it's a horrible plan, really.

Alvor must sense the danger he's in, for he moves his free hand over mine where it sits on his forearm. His thumb brushes over my knuckles, the warm caress sending goosebumps up my arm—which is luckily covered by my sleeve.

Abort mission. This was a bad plan.

What was I thinking?!

Alvor stares down at me, his eyebrow slowly raising. Why is it raising? What is he expecting from me?

Oh, yes. An answer.

I twist one of the curls that's fallen over my shoulder as I look away from Alvor and meet Lady Marian's inquisitive gaze. "It's fairly recent, and we're still adjusting to the reality of being able to see each other."

Lady Marian leans forward, a gleam in her eye. "Were you forbidden to court because of King Ferdinand?"

Alvor smirks. "Among other reasons."

Lady Marian gasps, her hand fluttering over her heart. "Oh, I do so love a romantic story with a happy ending, William. Don't you?" William opens his mouth to respond but shuts it again when Lady Marian leans across the table toward us. "Now tell me, Prince Alvor. Did you fake your death so you could be with your lady love? Is this why you were always so distant at court? Because your heart was already stolen by another?"

Alvor's eyes meet mine, humor dancing in his irises. "Lady Rowena has rescued me from a cruel fate. Faking my death was a small price to pay to live with her in my life. The love of a wonderful woman is more precious than any crown or rubies. Isn't that right, William?"

I want to cackle with how masterfully Alvor turned the tables on his cousin, drawing the attention away from us, but I settle for a demure smile. I do allow myself to squeeze Alvor's arm a little, not to feel his muscles—though they're nice—but rather to communicate my appreciation for his masterful social skills. His hand squeezes mine back.

We both look at Red, whose cheeks are pink, his eyes wide as he looks at Alvor. "Why yes, cousin, it's quite wonderful when you find a strong woman who knows her mind, and who allows you to join her in experiencing life."

Lady Marian sighs dramatically, leaning her head against Red's shoulder. "I'm so glad you decided to rob my father's carriage. This is the best day of my life."

Red blushes, and I hold in my snicker.

I let go of Alvor and pick up my spoon, taking a huge, unladylike bite of stew. Alvor chuckles, and then I watch as he does the same, letting his princely manners go and looking like one of my merry men. Conversely, Red is eating with the dignity he abandoned years ago.

What an entertaining group we are.

Lady Marian draws Red into conversation, but I block her out, my mind tired from the long day.

And let's be honest, I don't know how to make female friends . . . obviously.

I scrape my spoon on the bottom of my bowl when Marian says something that catches my attention.

"—with King Ferdinand wanting a new wife and all, it's been quite an uproar up at the castle. I think that's why Daddy decided I needed to be married off at the last minute. Something about keeping me away from the king."

Alvor's back straightens, his muscles tight. "The king is . . . what?"

Lady Marian's eyebrows raise. "Oh, I forgot. Of course you wouldn't know. Yesterday evening at dinner, King Ferdinand announced he's in search of a new wife. That he wants to marry and have more children. He said that in one week eligible young noblewomen are to come to the castle for a queenly competition, whatever that means."

Alvor's leg bounces with a speed that's concerning. I slip my hand under the table, setting it on his kneecap. He stills, though his body still vibrates with a palpable tension. His jaw clenches as his hands flex. "He doesn't need more children, Lady Marian. My father already has an heir."

Lady Marian's eyebrows draw together, her voice dropping to a gentle whisper devoid of her previous mirth. "But everyone thinks you're dead, Prince Alvor. To him, you are not an heir."

Alvor leans back, looking up at the sky for a brief moment before back down at his soup bowl. His hand travels under the table, sliding over mine and flipping it over, weaving our fingers together. He clings to me as much as I cling to him.

We're all quiet, and I'm grateful Lady Marian has picked up on Alvor's distress. I wouldn't be surprised if there's a cunning mind beneath that jovial façade she wears. Her eyes take in more than she says.

Alvor's knee bounces again, but I don't stop it this time. There's a crease between his brows, similar to the one he'd get during our studies as children, which means my job is to wait until he's chosen his next steps.

As much as I feel responsible for this kingdom and for caring for our people, I can't forget that Alvor is the real prince, his bloodline tied to the throne. Though he's technically still the prince, everything within our borders belongs to him.

Alvor's bouncing knee stills and his hand squeezes mine. He turns his head, his lips brushing against the tip of my ear as he whispers, "Rowena, I have a plan."

I nod. "Let's go."

He stands, his hand entwined with mine. I don't let go of his hand. Not as we get up and give our bowls to the washer girls, not as we silently signal my men to gather, and not as we wait until Red takes Lady Marian to the women's side of the camp. My fingers are wrapped around his for every minute, and I think I could get used to the warmth and connection the experience brings.

Alvor's grip is firm, anchoring me in the moment. If I wanted to pull my hand away, I could. He'd let go the minute he knew there was resistance—that's just who Alvor is.

Maybe it's the dress I'm still wearing. Maybe it's not having my scalp ache from having my hair pulled back in a tight braid. Or maybe, just maybe, I'm still holding Alvor's hand because I genuinely. . . like it.

As we gather around the merry men's campfire, I look around, and for once . . . I don't care what other people think about me and what I'm doing—because for the first time in a long time I feel wanted and safe.

And that's a feeling I'm going to continue fighting to keep.

Chapter Eighteen

A Plan Most Daring

Alvor

I'm clinging to Rowena's hand like it's a lifeline keeping me afloat. Which it is.

I'm drowning in guilt and fury. My mind is spinning, clinging to the threads of an idea that's taken hold and won't let go.

When Dale sits, the last to join us, Rowena turns to me. "What's your idea?"

I turn to the men. "Lady Marian informed us that my father desires to find another wife to produce a new heir for him now that his only heir is conveniently absent. This is a perfect opportunity for us to send in a spy."

I turn my gaze on Rowena, watching her until she puts the pieces together. Her nose wrinkles and her eyebrows raise, skepticism written across her face. "You want *me* to be the spy?"

The men let out a chorus of protests, and it's not until I raise my free hand that they quiet.

I squeeze Rowena's hand gently, running my thumb over her soft skin. "When you come to the castle, you're in your hunting leathers with your hair braided back and usually there's dirt or something on your face. But this look—" I swallow around the lump in my throat as I stare into her beautiful face. "You in a dress with your hair done. You're a lady, not a huntress, when you look like this."

Her lips purse. "I don't like it."

My stomach turns and I wince. "I know. But while you're at the ridiculous wedding competition, I can sneak through the castle, find my father's mirror, and work to break the enchantment."

Much speaks up from beside me. "You'll want magical help with that. If Robin isn't helping you destroy the mirror, then one of us should." He pauses to yawn. "We should also talk to Red's doctor uncle like we planned so he can help us know how to break the mirror and its curse."

My leg bounces, logistics unfolding in my mind. "Tomorrow morning we can visit Doc and then stay at William's estate."

Rowena raises her free hand. "Problem with that. They don't know he's alive."

I shrug. "Then it'll be a sweet family reunion. They'll find out soon enough. If they're in good spirits, they'll be more inclined to help us, and they could potentially sneak you into the queen competition. William's youngest sister hasn't been presented at court yet, so we could pretend that's who you are."

Rowena narrows her eyes. "So we're going to manipulate them into helping us by bringing their son back, and then putting them in danger by having them sneak us into the castle?"

I groan. "No. No manipulation. I'm not trying to con them into helping us. I just want to ask. If they say no, we'll find another way, Rowena."

Much yawns. "Good plan. I'm going to bed."

Everyone chuckles as he steps over to his hut, dragging his feet across the ground, though nobody else gets up to leave.

A weight lifts off my chest now that we have a plan of action.

Rowena stares into the flames in front of us until she squeezes my hand. "What are you going to do after you destroy the mirror?"

I stare into the fire. There's a wrestling match taking place in my heart. There's a hope that my father is under his own curse and will return to the good man of my younger years once it's broken. But then there's reality, and the fear that plagues me, whispering that my father is truly evil, that this curse is only amplifying the darkness already in his heart.

Either way, this has gone on too long.

"I'm going to confront him and take the throne. My father has abused it for too long. Even if he's cursed as I am, even if there's a good man beneath this darkness, our kingdom needs hope. They need a new ruler."

Stue raises his fist after a resounding sneeze. "Long live Prince Alvor."

The chant is quietly repeated by the other men, and I can't hold in the emotions any longer. I clench my jaw and squeeze my eyes shut, but a tear still leaks out and down my cheek.

"Planning meeting dismissed," Rowena says abruptly before pulling me to my feet and away from the group. I can barely see through the moisture in my eyes. We walk until I can make out her hut. She pushes aside the fur door and pulls me inside.

The fur falls closed behind me, blanketing us in darkness, and it's only then that I feel arms wrap around my waist. Rowena's head rests against my chest as she holds me tightly.

"Alvor," she whispers. "I'm sorry you have to do this. I'm sorry your father has been cursed." Her arms tighten around me, and I slowly lift mine, embracing her. Words fail me, and I let the tears fall into her loose curls.

Rowena holds me as my shoulders shake.

I mourn the loss of the father I grew up with, grief shredding my heart. My father wants me dead, and the betrayal hits me again.

Will I need to kill my father to take my throne? Can we do this without someone dying or getting hurt?

I don't know, and the unknown sits heavily on my chest as wretched sobs escape me.

When I crumple to the floor, Rowena sits and pulls my head into her lap. Her cool fingers run through my hair as my tears drench her skirt.

I'm numb and cold, the life I once knew dead and left behind at the edge of Sherwood Forest.

Chapter Nineteen

A Tear Most Cleansing

Rowena

I run my fingers through Alvor's silky strands, the color reminding me of the darkness seeping out of his eyes.

I noticed the first black tear back at the firepit with the men. My magic kicked in immediately, and as I led Alvor through the forest to my hut, my enhanced eyesight could see the streams of black trailing down his cheeks.

Alvor doesn't have magic, but I would guess that when a person chooses the light, it's just as magical as if someone were to manipulate the gift they've been given from Solwain.

Alvor blinks, his newest round of tears dripping down his face.

There's one important difference to these drops of liquid—they're clear.

My skirt is stained, but it doesn't matter, because finally—finally—Alvor is free of every last piece of inky darkness from his father's curse.

He reaches up, wiping a tear from his face. "I'm sorry."

I hold my hand up and let my magic run to the tips of my fingers, willing them to glow, just enough that he can see my face. The white light is comforting as it fills the small space. Dark blotches pepper my skirt underneath Alvor's head, but his face is clear, his eyes the full startling blue without a shadow in their depths.

I shake my head, my hair falling into his face before I pull it over my shoulder. "No, Alvor. You do not need to apologize. *I'm* sorry. I'm sorry I didn't save you earlier. I'm sorry I waited so long to do something beyond the bare minimum. You deserved someone to fight for you when you couldn't fight for yourself. How many times did I come to the castle in the past five years and purposefully avoid you because I felt slighted when really you were shrouded in darkness?"

There's a vise around my heart, squeezing until tears flow down my own cheeks.

Regret slithers through me as I think of the time I wasted moping and hiding away as I nursed my wounds, when I could have been saving him. Alvor. My best friend.

I hold up my hand, the light bathing Alvor's face. I reach out, tracing my finger from his eyebrows, down his cheek, to the stubble that hints of just how much he's grown since we were so close years ago. My voice hitches, a lump in my throat, but I swallow and talk through the emotions threatening to pull me under.

"Alvor, *you* changed overnight, and I didn't do *anything* about it when I knew the *real* you. The real you would have been more involved, more present, and you most definitely are not an airhead. The real you would have come and found me and forced me to talk to you. So this whole situation, if it is anyone's fault, is mine as well."

Alvor's hand comes up, gripping mine. He pulls my palm to his lips, placing a tender kiss against my skin. Goosebumps trail up my arm at his gentle touch, and I suck in a sharp breath, biting my bottom lip before I let out the sob threatening to overtake me.

"Rowena," he whispers. "We were so young. You were fifteen. The weight of our kingdom's survival was not meant to rest on your shoulders. I was only two years older than you. We were still children. Children mourning the losses of those closest to us." He places another kiss against my palm. "My mind is clearer than it's been in years. I can see back into the past with a clarity I've lacked. Neither of us is to blame, though we both could have made different decisions."

I sniffle and wipe my nose on my sleeve. Alvor chuckles and I scowl at him. "I'm not a lady, Alvor."

He arches his eyebrows, giving me that infuriatingly knowing look.

I roll my eyes, and it's only then that he sits up, crossing his legs beneath him. I rest my glowing hand on my legs, though he still has a hold of my other one. He twines our fingers together, and as I focus on that connection, my riotous emotions calm.

"I never stopped caring for you, though it seems those feelings were blocked for several years. Earlier, you implied we were courting in front of Lady Marian. Despite the problems we still need to solve with my father, I don't want that to be pretend. I want to court you, Rowena."

My heart leaps in my chest. The words I've been wanting to hear for years are finally being spoken by the man who's held my heart for just as long.

Our timing was never right, and despite the joy coursing through me, I know that now isn't the time for this either. "Alvor . . . we can't do this."

His face falls, and it's like an arrow to my heart, but falling in love during a rebellion is ridiculous. What if one of us doesn't make it by the end? Letting ourselves fall for each other will only lead to more pain.

Alvor's hand tightens around mine. "I respect your decision, and if you say this can't happen, then I won't push it. But I want you to know I'm serious about my feelings for you. I don't care if you're a huntress or an outlaw. You were my first friend, my first love, and you've been more of a leader to my kingdom over the past five years than I ever will be."

I shake my head, looking away so I don't give in. Because that's what I really want to do. I want to give in and stop fighting myself and my feelings.

But if I stop . . . then I'll just get hurt again.

Everyone I love has died, been cursed, or lives in squalor, and I'm just barely surviving as I try and do my best to fix it.

No. I can't let myself fall, because I don't know who will pick up the pieces if I break.

I squeeze my eyes shut. "I did what I had to do, princeling. That's it."

His hand comes up, his warm fingers chasing away the chill as they caress my jaw, gently turning my face until I can't look anywhere except for into his hypnotizing eyes.

"Drop your walls, Rowena. I know you call me 'princeling' when you're trying to put space between us. It's probably easier to pretend you're mad at me than admitting how you feel. But I'm not playing games. You just spent the last who knows how long comforting me while I cried into your skirt about everything I've gone through over the last days, months, and years. You can't fool me, sweetheart. You wouldn't have let me do that if you didn't like me."

I glare at him. He's right, and I can't make myself hate it. But I do hate one thing he just said. "Don't call me 'sweetheart.'"

He chuckles and lets go of my hand, pushing himself up off the floor. "You're right. Sweetheart doesn't quite fit for the outlaw who stole my heart."

I shake my head, turning my giggle into a scoff. I wave a hand in his direction, ready to be done with emotions tonight. "Good night, princeling."

He steps toward the door, pausing under the frame, a roguish grin that's illuminated by my magic highlighting every handsome angle of his face.

"Goodnight . . . Rowena."

It's only when the fur door covering falls back into place that I let myself fall into my bed, tears streaming down my cheeks as my imagination runs wild with dreams of things I fear can never be.

Chapter Twenty

A Village Most Poor

Alvor

"Princeling, it's time to go," Little John says as he shakes my arm.

I blink open my eyes to darkness.

"What?" My voice is raspy and my throat dry. There's a slight ache in my head, probably the result of crying last night.

"Come on," he urges. "We're going to go deliver the coins, remember?"

"Coins." I nod as I push myself up to a sitting position on my cot. "Deliver coins. Yup. Got it."

Little John grunts. "Don't take too long. Much and Stue are coming."

I nod and try to rub the sleep out of my eyes to no avail. I slip on my boots and shrug on my vest and cloak. I walk out of the hut only to be greeted by Much shoving a piece of fruit in my face.

"Eat it. It'll give you enough energy for the day. Dale and I made sure of that."

I nod my thanks as I take a bite of the peach, juice dribbling down my chin. I'm surprised to see Much awake and moving so quickly. He's like a sprite, hopping down the path toward the edge of the camp. Maybe a good night's sleep helps his magic replenish?

Ugh. I seriously need to learn more about magic.

Also magical creatures. Are there any left after Solwain left with his retinue? How do I know about creatures like sprites, but not if Solwain left behind more magical beings than just the magic he infused into some of the humans?

I kick a rock in the pathway harder than necessary as I rein in my grumblings about how my father has failed me.

It doesn't take me long to finish off the fruit in my hand, and by the time I do, I've caught up to Little John, Much, and Stue, who looks at me and then sneezes. Poor man's nose is red, and his eyes bloodshot.

Stue glares at me after I study his face for too long. "It's allergies, princeling. Now let's move." He spins around and stalks into the forest.

When I look over at Little John, he shrugs. He hefts one of the bags we packed the other night off the ground. "Think you can carry this?"

I smile. "If I couldn't, I wouldn't tell you."

Little John grunts, this one sounding almost like a laugh. "Good man."

I nod, taking the proffered bag and masking my reaction at its weight.

There is no way I'm going to complain about carrying this to a village. Today I choose to do the hard things, to accept the challenges that will stretch me.

Plus, I'm supposed to be a trained knight, even if Father never let me officially become one because it was "too dangerous as his heir."

This bag will be the perfect way to start training.

I should have never skipped training.

I'm not weak, but carrying an awkward-sized bag full of coins as you run through the forest first thing in the morning would have anyone's arms shaking. Mine tremble as I heft the bag a little higher, securing it on my shoulder as we study the outskirts of Nottingham village. It's close enough to our capital city and the castle that the people receive much of my father's wrath, though far enough removed that I'm not familiar with the layout or the people.

Stue stops in front of me before turning and beckoning us to gather in a close huddle. His voice drops to a whisper. "Much, I want you to sneak around and see if any of the king's men are in the area, specifically if any tax collectors are here. The rest of us are going to the village elder's house. He'll know which families need this the most."

Much nods, pulls up his hood, and practically bounces away, flitting through the shadows as he slinks into the town that's just barely waking up. Few people walk the streets, and those who do seem to carry the weight of the world on their shoulders.

My heart twists in my chest, seeing the dark circles under their eyes, their gaunt figures, and their threadbare clothing.

My father did this. Though is it really him? Or is it the curse?

I shove away the frustrating feelings and tug on my hood, pulling it farther down my face as we enter into town. Stue and Little John walk ahead of me, weaving through alleyways like experienced thieves, or should

I say, bandits. We're quietly making our way through the village, heading toward the center of town, when a small noise catches my attention.

A tiny sneeze coming from behind a stack of crates has my feet slowing. There's a brief shuffling noise before it's quiet again. Little John turns around, eyebrows raised, but I hold up my hand and point toward the crates. Little John walks back to me and I hand him my bag before slowly inching around the wooden boxes.

There, tucked into the space between the crates and building, is a little boy. His eyes are wide when they meet mine, his shaggy hair falling into his face. His clothes hang on his body, and as he wipes his nose on his torn sleeve, I see some fire light up his eyes.

"Whatcha want, mister?" he growls.

I crouch in front of him, studying the boy who I'd guess is around age eight. "I'm curious and would like to know what you're doing behind these crates."

He looks at the ground, no longer meeting my eyes. "Hiding."

I nod. "I gathered as much. What, or rather whom, are you hiding from?"

He looks up at me, his nose wrinkling. "You be using a lot of fancy words, mister."

I shrug. "I like fancy words. I'd also like to know who you're hiding from."

The boy shifts in the dirt, not meeting my eyes again. He picks at a thread at the hem of his pant leg. "Momma said I needed to find my own food. She can't afford to feed me anymore with all of the taxes. But I don't want to steal, and I don't know where to get food . . . so I'm here."

My eyes sting, but I blink away the moisture threatening to escape at his simple statement. "What—" I swallow, clearing away the lump in my throat before I start again. "What's your name?"

"Caleb."

I turn, looking over my shoulder, only to see Little John already holding out his hand with one of the coin packs. He tosses it to me, and I catch it before holding it out to Caleb.

"Well, Caleb. I applaud your desire not to steal. You have an integrity about you that is to be commended. Your mother has raised a fine young man. So why don't you go on home and give your momma these coins."

Caleb's eyes go wide, his gaze riveted on the small cloth package in my hand. "But, sir . . ."

I shake my head. "No buts. Now go on home. But Caleb," —I pause, waiting until his eyes meet mine— "if you ever need food and can't find any, head into the woods and look for Robin Hood. His band of merry men will take care of you. I'm hoping life will change soon for our kingdom, but until then, you can find refuge with Robin."

Caleb looks around furiously before his voice goes even quieter. "But Robin Hood is a bandit, sir."

I smile. "I know. But Robin Hood takes care of this kingdom, unlike King Ferdinand. He'll take care of you."

Caleb frowns. "Momma says stealing ain't right."

I lean forward, ruffling his hair and dropping the coins in his lap. "She's right, and I can't say I'm happy that Robin Hood steals from the rich to feed the poor. But I can say I'm grateful he redistributes the king's wealth to those who need it."

Caleb looks down at the coins in his lap. "I'm right confused, sir."

My shoulders slump. "So am I, young man. But it's a discussion to be continued on another day. We must be going, and you have a job to do. Go back to your momma, young Caleb. I'm sure she'll be happy to see you."

Caleb pushes himself up and tucks the bag of coins into his pocket, his hand gripping it tightly. "Thank you, sir." He bobs his head and I step back, watching as he emerges from his hiding place and races down the dirt path.

Little John grunts from behind me. "We going to go?"

"Is this how it is in the other villages?"

"Do you really want me to answer that?"

I shake my head. "No. I already know."

He hands me my bag, and we hurry to catch up to Stue, who glares at us from the end of the alley.

We slip into the back door of the village elder's home, and Stue exchanges quiet words with the man. I can't stop thinking about Caleb and his family. My mind is caught up, imagining the agony of Caleb's mother, who had to send away her own son because she couldn't feed him. Because of my father's greed.

As we slip back out and begin leaving small packets of coins in windowsills and tucked under doors, all I can do is imagine that each home belongs to Caleb's family. Each one filled with young children desperate for their next meal.

With each building, each door with paint peeling off of it, each cracked window, all I can see is Caleb's gaunt face.

Our adventure takes all morning, as we stay in the shadows and out of sight. By the time we slip out of Nottingham, it's lunch time, and I'm exhausted.

But the thought of eating food has my stomach turning. How can I eat when my people are starving?

Chapter Twenty-One

A Heart Most Tender

Rowena

My eyes are puffy, and my hair takes longer to detangle before I braid it out of my face. The sun is already up, but I'm not in a rush. The men are probably still in the village delivering the goods we stole from Lady Marian's father. Even if they left without me to go see Red's doctor uncle, I wouldn't really care. I could catch up with them if I wanted.

But I know they won't leave me behind. At least Alvor won't.

There's a bowl of porridge on the floor by the door, and I step over, picking it up. It's cooled, but it'll still taste good if Dale had anything to say about it. Is he the one who slipped it into my hut? Probably him or Little John. They tend to be the most tender, despite their gruff exteriors.

I slurp down my porridge and move to finish getting dressed.

I slip on my leather jerkin and tighten the laces at the sides, then run through my weapons checklist.

Quiver? Check.

Daggers in my boots? Check.

Dagger on my waist? Check.

Desire to cry because I don't know whether I should throw myself in Alvor's arms or whether I should keep my distance? Check.

It was a long night.

I don't know what possessed me to bring him to my hut, but somehow I just sensed he needed a good cry. My magic knew his needs.

With the tears that he shed, the last of the darkness seeped out of him. It left his body, light filling him up until all I could see was the Alvor of our youth.

Which is why I couldn't say yes. Why I pulled back.

Because that Alvor, *he's the king*. The rightful ruler. No matter my secrets, he needs to marry someone strong who will bring light back to the kingdom. My magic might be made up of light, but I've also stolen from others and broken the law for years. So being a queen?

Yeah.

That's *not* for me.

When this is over, I'm going to simply fade away. I'll travel, take care of the forest like Solwain taught us to, and care for the poor and needy. No responsibilities that would take me to the castle where the ghosts of my parents haunt me and the unattainable mocks me.

I take one last deep breath before I walk out of my hut, clipping my cloak around my shoulders and pulling my hood up over my braid. Lady Marian is somewhere around here with Red, and I do not want to talk about why Robin Hood is, in fact, a female.

Lady Marian's laugh rings out through the morning and I pivot, changing directions and glancing around until I find a familiar face. The young woman giggles again, a feat I'm surprised she's able to accomplish after sleeping on a cot, but her stamina and backbone is to be commended. She has grit, which is something I can respect.

Okay, Lady Marian is growing on me. Especially since she's claimed Red as her intended bandit and hasn't tried to go after Alvor.

Not that I would have been jealous, or that I'm feeling possessive.

Okay, I am feeling possessive, which is a feeling I need to get rid of and soon, because I don't like being mad at other women, especially over a man. It just feels wrong. We're to support each other, not trade barbed remarks.

I shake my hands at my side and look around for one of my men.

Dale finds me first, popping up at my side. "You didn't get breakfast." He frowns, and I pat his shoulder.

"Actually, someone brought me some. I needed a little bit of extra space this morning."

He nods, and we walk in silence down the well-worn path toward the edge of camp and away from Red and Lady Marian.

I tilt my head toward Dale. "Did the others go to Nottingham this morning?"

"Yup. Left early like you said to. Little John thinks they won't be back until after the noon meal."

I nod, kicking a pebble on the pathway. "I better check in with Cook again. If I'm gone too long, there might be questions."

He looks over, meeting my eyes. "You sure you want to go back there, Robin? You could always disappear like the rest of us."

A sigh escapes my lips. "I wish I could, Dale. But how else am I to keep tabs on our illustrious monarch? Plus, I can't go without Cook's sweet rolls; you know that."

He chuckles, one of the few times I've actually heard him laugh. "It's hard to make those out here, isn't it?"

I clap his shoulder again. "You know we would have starved long ago without your efforts. Between you and Much, we've actually been able to keep everyone healthy and well fed."

He shrugs. "It's nothing."

My breath hitches. "No, Dale. It's more than nothing; it's everything to these people. It's everything to me. You could have left Lyriva long ago, gone to another kingdom where you would have been paid handsomely for your magical skills. Maybe even met a pretty lady, but instead . . . instead you stayed."

He scoffs. "I'm not a saint, Robin."

"No, but you're pretty close."

He shakes his head again, a wry smile on his lips. "Away with you. Go find something to take to Cook. We don't need any of your flattery around here."

I jog ahead before turning around, running backward for a moment as I yell, "Thank you, Dale!"

He waves a hand in the air, dismissing me as he turns back to camp. I chuckle as I weave into the brush, letting my magic unfurl around me and soaking in the moment of peace.

My heart wasn't in the hunt today. The few pheasants tied to my waist are a testament to how little effort I put into my job.

But Cook doesn't seem to mind as I bring in my catch of the day. Her eyes light up, a smile tugging at her lips before she schools her expression. "Girl, what are you doing here?"

She snaps her fingers and points to the corner of the kitchen, where she shoos some of the prep cooks away. I set down the birds and Cook gets right to pulling out their feathers. I join her, the methodical action taming my heart's rapid beating.

"I'm doing my job, bringing you meat like the good huntress I am."

She squints. "A good huntress would be far away from here with a certain someone who needs to avoid this castle."

I glare right back. "Why? Why do I need to avoid being here?"

Cook huffs. "You know why, girl. Don't sass me. You can see it just like I can."

I lower my voice. "See what?"

Cook shakes her head. "You want me to join you on a hunt? I can't say anything. There are ears everywhere."

I nod. "Can you tell me more about this quest for a wife the king is on?"

She rolls her eyes. "It's a hullaballoo—that's what it is. But I'll be cooking up a feast all of next week in preparation. Seems we need a new queen after ten years of not having one. I pity the poor woman he chooses."

"Any ideas who the king wants?"

Cook shakes her head. "Now that Lady Marian has disappeared under mysterious circumstances, I don't have a clue. The other women of noble birth have stopped attending court, which is why a mandatory summons for each noble family was sent out today. Every family must have one eligible maiden attend the competition for the queen's throne. Unless there are none available, in which case a representative from the family must pay a hefty sum to the king."

My eyebrows raise. "More gold?"

Cook's only response is a nod as she moves from one plucked bird to the next. Her hands still, her gray eyes staring into mine, their color matching the hairs at her temples. "Girl, you know I don't want to see you hurt. Leave. Leave while you can."

My hands fist at my side, my voice a low hiss. "You know I can't." I look around the kitchen, at the morose maids, cooks, and men walking through the room. "How can I when I can do something about this?"

She plucks a feather, pointing it at me. "The world needs your light, girl. Don't lose it."

I tap my fingers on the tabletop. "I have a plan."

She squints. "You better have more than one. You never know what's going to happen."

I sigh. "You're right."

My eyes are drawn to the door, a tug in my chest bringing with it a memory of blue eyes that I haven't seen all day.

I shove that thought down.

I am not a woman to daydream about a man's eyes. Who has time for that? Not me. Cook just said I need more than one plan to overthrow the king. I can't be daydreaming about Alvor at a time like this.

"Go, my girl," Cook whispers, a small smile on her lips. "Go find him. Make plans, but be safe."

I haven't had a mother in ten years, but in this moment, as I look into Cook's misting gaze, I can't help but admit how much this woman has come to mean to me.

There's a yell from the hallway leading into the castle depths. Cook's eyes widen, and she points to the door. "Go."

I nod, slipping to the edge of the room and sliding against the wall as I make a quick escape.

I do not want to see King Ferdinand today, not when he's bellowing at servants like that.

I've had enough of faking people's deaths for a lifetime.

Chapter Twenty-Two

An Encounter Most Flirtatious

Alvor

I stumble into camp, Much and Stue behind me. Little John mumbled something about horses for Robin before breaking off from our group on our way back, but I don't have the energy to care.

I've never been more tired in my life. These past few days have been exhausting, emotionally and physically. After seeing the state of Nottingham . . . well, I can't deny that I'm ready to march into the castle and take the throne for myself already.

But we need to have a plan. I don't want any bloodshed, and I don't want to have to fight my people who are under a curse.

We have to figure this out, and soon. I can't take seeing hungry children for much longer.

Heads turn toward us as we enter the clearing where Dale is serving lunch.

He doesn't say a word, just arches his eyebrows at us.

Yeah, I probably don't look too happy right now, but I can't seem to wipe the scowl from my face.

William and Lady Marian stand up from where they're sitting and walk toward me. William's eyebrows lower. "Did something happen? Where's Little John?"

I shake my head. "Nothing happened besides me seeing the horrible life my father has inflicted upon our people. Little John disappeared a while back. Something about horses and finding Row—Robin."

My eyes flick to Lady Marian who squints at me, as if there's something she's puzzling out. "You look different today, Prince Alvor."

I nod. "I should hope so. I'm a completely different person now than I was even a day ago."

She shakes her head. "No, it's more than that. Yes, being an outlaw and living with bandits changes you. I mean, my hair is in a simple braid this morning, and I'm having stew for lunch. No. There is more to your changes. Your eyes are brighter." She steps forward, getting uncomfortably close as she stares into my face. "Your eyes were darker. They've always been blue, but now they're bright, as if filled with light."

I let out a breath when she steps back. "That's probably because my father's cursed magic is gone. Row—Robin used magic to help rid me of the rest of it somehow."

Lady Marian quirks an eyebrow. "Robin Hood must be very powerful, then. I'd really like to meet the man, if you can track him down."

Movement on the edge of the clearing catches my attention. Rowena's eyes meet mine before flitting away as she sprints toward the huts. "I'm sure you'll meet Robin Hood eventually, Lady Marian. For now, there's someone I need to talk to."

She turns to William. "There are a lot of secrets in this camp, Red. I cannot wait until I unravel them all."

He grins. "There are. One day I'll tell you about all of them."

She sighs, leaning her head on his shoulder. "Alright, I guess I can be patient."

William nods at me and turns away. I slip past the couple and head toward the hut, trailing far behind Rowena. By the time I get to her place, she's emerging, her dress from last night on, dark stains on the skirt.

"Are we ready to go to Red's uncle?" she asks as she finishes pulling her hair over her shoulder, her fingers deftly weaving the strands into a loose braid.

"I don't know. It might be too late today."

Her nose wrinkles, her freckles pronounced with the motion. I take a step closer, my fingers itching to trace the patterns on her cheeks. She looks up, and I'm mesmerized by how her dress brings out the green in her eyes.

"It might be too late to travel that far north today. Unless you wanted to get there in the dark, but I imagine you'd rather travel while there's light out."

Her eyebrows arch. "The sun doesn't set for a while during the summer. I think we can make it."

"Rowena, we can go tomorrow morning."

She folds her arms. "We should go tonight. The sooner we get answers from someone who knows things, the better. We're floundering here, Alvor. I don't know how to break the curse. We have less than a week until this queen's contest, and every day more of our people are going hungry and suffering."

I reach out, gently gripping her elbows, and pull her closer to me. My hands slip down her arms until my fingers interlace with hers. "Rowena," I whisper. "There's no point in pushing ourselves more than we need to. A trip to William's estate will take the rest of the day if we're on foot. We can leave in the morning. I, for one, need some time after visiting Nottingham. Yes, there is much we need to accomplish, but for once, can you stop thinking about everyone else and consider yourself? You've been running through the woods for days. You need time to recover. We all do. We can work on making a better plan tonight with the men."

She glares at me. "The best way to take care of myself is to take care of everyone else."

I shake my head. "No. That's the best way for you to fail, Rowena. You've been doing that for years. The burden is mine. Share it with me."

Her shoulders slump and she leans forward, resting her forehead against my chest. "I don't know how, Alvor. How do I let it go? How do I keep it from plaguing my mind every minute of the day?"

I wrap my arms around her, gently rubbing circles against her back. "If I knew, I'd tell you."

She snorts. "So how are you supposed to share my burden if you don't know how I'm supposed to give it up?"

I shrug. "I don't know, it just sounded right, and romantic, so I said it."

Rowena laughs, a sound I haven't heard in years. The noise fills my soul, and I tighten my embrace, treasuring this moment in the midst of the depths of emotions we're both facing.

She leans her head back, a twinkle in her eye. "You sure know how to win the ladies, Alvor."

I lean down, placing a kiss on her forehead. "The only lady I want to win is you, Rowena."

Her mouth drops open for a second before snapping shut. "There he is, the swoony Prince Alvor."

"Swoony? I didn't know you could feel such emotions."

Those beautiful hazel eyes of hers roll up to the sky. "As if you don't know you're handsome, Alvor."

"Do you think I'm handsome, Rowena?"

She shakes her head and pushes out of my arms. "If you're just going to fish for compliments, then we're going to be done here."

I snatch her hand up before she steps too far away from me. "Never fishing, just coveting." I lift her hand to my lips, placing a kiss on her knuckles. A blush spreads across her cheeks.

She blinks twice before yanking her hand out of mine. "Yeah, okay. We're done here. Let's go see what the camp needs our help with if we're not going to Red's home tonight."

A chuckle escapes me as I trail behind her, the skirts of her dress billowing with each of her long strides.

As we enter the clearing, I hear the sound of hooves. Rowena stops in front of me as we both turn to see Little John riding into camp, a string of horses behind him.

A rare smile graces his face as he dismounts in front of Rowena.

"What are these for, Little John?"

His grin widens. “You’re not the only one with tricks up your sleeve, Robin. I thought we might want to travel in style to Red’s home, which means horses.”

Rowena turns to me and smirks. “Guess we are going tonight.”

I bow my head. “As you wish, m’lady.”

Chapter Twenty-Three

A Doctor Most Surprised

Rowena

We travel in silence, weaving through the woods on our mounts until we come upon the road leading to Red's estate in the northernmost area of Lyriva. It's an hour past the evening meal, but there are still people milling about the town as we enter it. I pull my hood farther down, though I don't know why I need to disguise myself while I'm still in this ridiculous skirt. I should have changed before we left, but with Lady Marian accompanying us, I couldn't justify it.

Pants would have been more comfortable with this saddle, but Little John wasn't thinking about that when he "borrowed" these horses. I'm still unsure if he stole them or did, in fact, borrow them. They're not the king's mounts, and the tack doesn't have any markings on it.

I guess I can let the man have some secrets; I still have at least one up my sleeve.

Red maneuvers to the front of our group, leaving Lady Marian at the back with Little John. Red's hood is low, but he weaves through the streets with an experience I envy.

I'm only marginally good at riding horses. I'd prefer to walk or run. But since I let my magic connect me with my mount, it's been a smoother ride as I've been able to read his moods. The gelding is a good choice for me, and I'd compliment Little John on it if I didn't think it'd make him insufferable.

Red hunkers down over the neck of his mount for a moment as we pass a large group of people, before he stops in front of a larger building. He dismounts, and I follow suit before tying our horses to the hitching post.

It's a very nice building with a covered walkway and with several chairs facing the road, the front entrance farther back from the dirt path. I look back and only Alvor has dismounted. Little John rides forward with Marius and Lady Marian beside him.

Marius grins at me. "We'll go find some lodging for the evening and get our guest a meal while you all . . . discuss things."

Lady Marian smiles, relieving my guilt at leaving the woman alone. "Oh wonderful, I've been meaning to ask you about some of your songs, Marius."

"I'll be happy to play some for you."

Alvor steps up beside me, his hand going to my lower back as he ushers me toward the door. "They'll be fine," he whispers.

A sigh escapes me. "I know. I just . . . worry."

He doesn't laugh at my statement, which I appreciate; instead, his thumb brushes up my spine, a gentle caress that makes me shiver. "You're a good leader, Rowena."

I duck my head, words escaping me, which is just fine because Red is holding the door open for us, a smirk across his lips. I narrow my eyes at him, and he only chuckles before walking into the building.

We walk into a large room. Empty chairs line the walls, and at the back of the room is a small table by a door. A middle-aged woman sits there, knitting needles flying. Her eyes stay focused on her task as she greets us. "Doctor will be right with you."

Red walks up to the table and crouches down until his head is on her same level. He waits until she looks up and meets his eyes before saying anything. "Hey, Aunt Marny, guess who's back."

The woman's eyes are wide, her knitting needles frozen in place before they fall from her hands. She reaches across the table, pulling Red into a tight embrace. "William, my boy. Oh, how we've worried about you. They said you died, but I couldn't ever believe it. Your parents didn't either. But my boy, why haven't you come home sooner?"

Aunt Marny doesn't let go of him; in fact, her grip tightens as she spews more questions. Then suddenly, she pushes him away. "You ridiculous boy, you've been alive this entire time? You couldn't have told any of us where you went?" She smacks him upside the head before hugging him again. "Oh, it's so good to see you."

The door to the back room opens. A man, about the same age as the woman walks out. "Marny, what's all the fuss about?"

He stops just past the doorframe, stock-still, and I take the opportunity to study him. The man is an older image of Red, with white streaking his curly auburn hair. He has the same straight nose, square jaw, broad shoulders, and tapered waist as his nephew. If I didn't already know who Red's father was, I would guess it was this man. The familial resemblance is absolutely uncanny.

Red steps out of Marny's embrace. "Hello, Uncle."

The man's chin quivers and he reaches out, pulling Red into his arms. The men are silent for a moment, until Red's uncle pushes back, hands going to frame Red's face. "How did this happen? We thought you were dead, William. We weren't sure what the king did to you, but you didn't come back. You didn't come back for *three years.*"

Red nods. "I know. There was a good reason I didn't come back. But now I'm here, and we have a plan to fix things with the king."

The doctor's eyes turn to us, and when he sees Alvor his mouth drops open a fraction. If the man weren't a doctor, I'd be worried about his heart from all the shocking announcements of the evening. "I see. Why don't you all come back to my office, and we'll discuss what this is all about."

We nod and file into the back room that's surprisingly empty.

The doctor stays at the door. "Marny, please don't let anyone interrupt us unless it's a life-or-death situation. We're about ready to close for the night anyway."

Marny's voice rings out, a slight waver to her tone. "Of course, dear. Take all the time you need."

He nods and closes the door. The man gestures to a few vacant chairs. Alvor's hand comes up, resting against my back again as he leads me to the seats. I miss his touch when he sits down beside me.

I watch Alvor as he straightens his shoulders, a mask of neutrality covering his emotions. It's the mask of Prince Alvor—a mask I've hated for years.

Except that Alvor was cursed. The one before me is not.

Red's uncle pulls up a stool, sitting across from the three of us.

Alvor clears his throat. "Doctor, thank you for meeting with us."

He waves his arm. "Standford. My first name is Standford. William's mother is my sister. I can assume you both have something to do with William surviving, so we shall not stand on ceremony here."

Alvor nods. "Thank you, Standford. We've come because I'd like to overthrow my father's rule and assume the throne. He cannot be trusted to run our kingdom any longer."

Standford grunts and folds his arms. "About time. How can I help?"

Alvor turns to me, nudging me with his elbow. I let out a breath and lower my hood. Standford doesn't bat an eye at my appearance nor my gender, and I'm grateful for it. "King Ferdinand was given a mirror. The mirror is enchanted, but not in a good way. I think it's cursed, and the king is helping spread its darkness throughout the kingdom. When the king speaks, the curse spreads. Prince Alvor was cursed and shed the rest of the lingering effects of the darkness last night."

I pause, the emotions from the evening prior washing over me again. "The curse is pure darkness, a blackness that has corrupted the king, his court, and our kingdom."

Standford nods, his face showing no signs of surprise. "I believe you. There are a few who have traveled to me for healing from the capital. Those who have—well, their treatments have been . . . harder. It feels more like a fight to get them to relax and accept the healing."

I clasp my hands together in my lap, resisting the urge to grip my skirt. "Re—William mentioned that you attended the academy. We were wondering if you knew anything about breaking curses or enchantments? Maybe some knowledge that could help us destroy the mirror? To rid ourselves of the darkness?"

Standford runs his fingers through his curls, a movement so familiar it's as if I'm seeing Red's double. His brows furrow as he stares at the floor for a moment. "The opposite of darkness is light. That's the basics of Solwain's gift. Objects can be enchanted by fusing someone's light magic into it. Cursed objects are made when someone imbues the worst of themselves into the item." He sighs before looking up into my eyes. "Someone who has twisted their gift, who uses it to bring others down, to destroy, demean, or deceive, can put those desires into an object if they were previously blessed with that gift. Very few have the ability to enchant objects, and those who do are usually watched diligently because of the risk if they were to choose a path of darkness."

Standford stares at the floor again. "Enchanting an object with light is easy, but to imbue dark magic they would need to inscribe ancient runes with a drop of their blood onto the item. It's forbidden magic. Only briefly mentioned at the Academy of Radiance, just enough to warn us against using it. From what I remember, to break the curse, someone with strong light magic will need to touch the object and place a drop of their blood onto it. Then they'll channel their light magic into the item until it conquers the darkness."

Standford's gaze returns to mine. "Miss, you seem to have the strongest light magic of us all. I can sense it radiating off of you. You would be a good choice to destroy the mirror."

My skin crawls at the idea, but he's not wrong. I have the strongest magic amongst my merry men.

Alvor clenches his fists in his lap, his entire body tense. "Can't we choose someone else?"

Standford tilts his head. "Prince Alvor, light combats dark. Whatever her magic specialty is, it's very much filled with light. My magic is second to her strength. I can sense her magic from where I'm sitting, which is unusual for me. Normally, I sense a person's magic when I'm touching them. William's magic is half as strong as mine, and gives him extra stamina. As far as I know, young prince, you don't possess any magical abilities. Which means she will be key to your success, if you choose to try and break the cursed object."

I place my hand on Alvor's shoulder. "It's fine," I whisper. "I've been in this fight for a long time; what's a little bit of blood on a mirror going to do to me?"

He shakes his head. "I don't like it, Rowena. It should be me."

I shrug, burying my worries deep within me. "Well it's not. We'll have to sneak me into the castle, and I can use the—" I bite my tongue before I spill my secret about the tunnels. "—the hallways to get to your father's chambers and break the mirror. Easy as pie."

Alvor narrows his eyes. "You don't like pie."

"Today I do."

Alvor's dark hair flops into his eyes, and my fingers twitch with the desire to move the strands back into place. "I still don't like it."

I arch my eyebrows. "Doesn't matter, princeling. It's happening."

Alvor opens his mouth, ready to call me out on his nickname, but Standford rises from his stool and walks over to his desk, pulling out a quill and parchment. "I'll write down what I remember for you to study. You cannot forget a step."

I shiver at the thought of the gaudy gold mirror sitting in King Ferdinand's room. I really don't want to touch that thing. "Are you sure I have to put a drop of blood onto it?"

Standford looks up from what he's writing, his face solemn. "I'm sure. The light is inside of you. It's a part of you. By sacrificing a part of yourself and your light, it's a sign you're willing to fight off the darkness. Many don't talk about how living a life filled with light means sacrificing the easy choices of falling into anger, lies, and unkindness. Our magic requires strength. It's a fight for the light, and this is but another example of it."

My shoulders sag, and I lean back into my chair. I've never thought about my magic in this way. But Standford is not wrong. Some days it's easy to enjoy my magic, which flows effortlessly. Other days, it's hard to access when I let the darkness of the world worm its way into my heart. Many of my hunting choices are made to help prevent an animal's suffering. Many times, I've chosen the harder right decision and gotten into fights to protect others. But every time I've chosen the light, every time I've chosen the goodness, it's been worth it.

Each sacrifice is worth it.

Putting Alvor on the throne is worth it.

Chapter Twenty-Four

An Arrival Most Unexpected

Alvor

I want to rip the paper Rowena is folding out of her hands. Instead, I watch as she tucks it into her dress, as if that seals the decision that she'll be the one to sacrifice a drop of her precious blood to break the curse.

Unkind words run through my mind, aimed at Doctor Standford even though I know he's not the true recipient of my ire.

But there's only a dark void in my mind and heart when I think about my father, a swirling pool of betrayal and hurt I'm not ready to dive into . . . yet.

William stands, drawing my attention away from Rowena.

"Thank you, Uncle. We're heading up to the estate, if you'd like to join us."

Doctor Standford smiles. "Oh, how I'd love to see the reunion, but I should stay. Don't want to bring too much attention to your arrival if your plan is to remain beneath everyone's notice."

William nods, and the two fall into a quiet conversation as we walk toward the front of the building. Standford shakes my hand before I exit, and though I'm grateful we came here and learned more about the curse, I can't say I'm pleased.

I step onto the front porch and watch as William gives another hug to his aunt.

We walk to our horses, and I help Rowena up into her saddle. She shoots me a playful glare.

Yes, she could do it herself.

No, I won't let her.

Somebody needs to take care of our fearless leader.

It's me. I'm the somebody.

We trot down the lane, William leading us closer to where the village ends and his family estate begins.

The buildings thin, and Marius waves us down when we turn a corner.

Marius holds up a roll in his hand as we approach. He hands a roll to Rowena, and then to me. Lady Marian approaches William, who dismounts to talk to her.

"Find a place to stay?"

Marius sighs. "No, actually. Which means we might need to beg for lodging with Red's family."

William looks over. "It should be no problem; there were always plenty of empty rooms growing up, I'm sure we can fit everyone there."

Little John frowns. "Are you sure? I feel having several unannounced guests will become fast spreading gossip, Red."

William shrugs. “We’re almost to the end of everything, right? My family and servants can be discreet.”

Lady Marian smiles, her voice demure. “I wouldn’t mind sleeping in a real bed.”

William grins, a besotted look on his face. “Then it’s decided, we’re going home.”

He pulls his hood back up, helps Lady Marian remount, and by the time I’m done eating my sweet roll, we’re on our way again.

There’s not much distance to cross between here and the castle William grew up in, but soon enough he’s urged his horse into a gallop. Rowena looks over with a worried glance before urging her horse to go faster.

The short ride is exhilarating, but the closer we get to the stone building, the more a pit grows in my stomach. I haven’t seen it since I was young. The darkness from earlier swirls inside, urging me to fall into its depths.

My mother took me here once to visit her brother and his children. It’s one of my first memories of playing with William and his two younger sisters. I was always jealous he had siblings.

Being an only child was lonely. It meant playing with the other children at court. My eyes stray to the one person who was always at court with me, the one I spent the most time with.

Rowena.

The spires appear atop the towers on each side of the castle. Towers we raced up and down while pretending to be guards at the ripe young age of six. It was fun to have another boy my age. William and I were best friends.

Why didn’t we come here more often?

I ride up closer to William's horse. Lady Marian leads hers a few feet away, and I give her a grateful nod.

"William, did your parents ever tell you why I didn't come visit more often? My mother never gave me a straight answer when I was younger, and when she passed, I stopped caring about it."

William's smile dims. "Alvor, my mother has magic. Her whole side of the family does. It's a very prominent part of the way we run our estate and care for our tenants. Father always told me he worried about your mother. Your parents married for love, but the king always seemed to keep you and your mother isolated at court. Your father's distaste for my family became apparent when my magic manifested when we were eight. That's when the visits stopped. If I wanted to see you, I had to come to court. We stopped coming except for when Father needed to for council meetings."

The unending rage and hurt flames to life inside my chest. The constant question I avoid thinking about flits through my mind.

Is my father cursed? Or does he enjoy spreading darkness?

My hands tighten on the reins before I loosen them, giving my horse its head again. "Was I blind, William? How did I not see his manipulations?"

William looks at me, compassion lining his face. "You were a child, Alvor. Then a teenager who lost his mother. How were you expected to recognize the signs of a tyrant seizing power?"

How indeed?

I pull my horse back, falling behind him and the rest of our entourage until I'm next to Rowena again.

Our horses slow as we reach the gate leading up to the castle. A guard steps forward, stopping in front of William, brandishing his spear. "State your business."

William turns his horse to the side and drops his hood. I can't see his face, but I'd guess he smiles mischievously as he says, "The prodigal son has returned."

The guard's mouth falls open.

There's grumbled mumbling from Rowena who urges her horse forward enough that she can lean over and yank William's hood back on his head.

She stares down at the guard. "We'd like an audience with Duke and Duchess Scarlett, please. As you can see, there is an important matter of a sensitive nature that needs to be discussed." She pauses, her voice lowering menacingly. "I would advise you to keep the information to yourself."

The guard stationed farther away from us turns and heads into the castle while the one Rowena has intimidated bows his head and gestures for us to enter the courtyard.

We ride into the mostly empty area. A handful of stable boys greet us, grabbing our reins and taking the horses away. We're drawing attention, but I don't know what I expected when two women and four men—one of which is the living heir of the estate—magically arrive on the castle doorstep.

William loops Lady Marian's arm through his, and I take Rowena's, treasuring the brief contact as we walk up to the front of the castle doors. A butler rushes out of the doors and immediately spies William. Tears mist over his eyes. He opens and closes his mouth like a fish before words finally come out. "Lord William, please follow me to your mother's sitting room. Your family anxiously awaits to see if you are, in fact, r-real."

He bows and scurries back inside.

William chuckles. "This should be entertaining," he murmurs to Lady Marian, who smiles up at him.

As we walk in, we all shed our hoods, handing our capes to a maid who greets us in the entryway. We walk at a languid pace, William leading our group through the entrance hall until he stops at a closed door. Judging from the location, it's one of the sitting rooms and has a nice view of the gardens on the side of the castle.

William stops, his hand on the door handle. Lady Marian wraps her arm around his waist. Rowena pulls from my hold and steps forward, hugging the other side of William.

Rowena whispers, "You can do this. It's been a long time, but they love you."

My heart aches for my cousin. Mourning a loss is not for the weak.

If it were my mother on the other side of this door, I know I'd be filled with a mix of joy and grief over the years we've lost. If she were secretly alive the whole time, there might be a hint of bitterness in those feelings too.

Maybe that's what William is afraid of.

Rowena turns her head, resting it on William's shoulder so that she can see me. Her eyes are misty. Of all of us, she's lost the most.

Is this moment reminding her of her own demons? Her own grief?

Our mothers died on the same day. Is she also imagining what it'd be like to have her parents on the other side of the door?

Marius steps around me, his hand resting on William's shoulder, blocking my view of Rowena. "This will be a tale I'll happily spread when the time is right. The beautiful reunion of Red the bandit, who sheds the mask of his past to return to the Scarlett Castle in triumph."

William chuckles, which breaks the tender moment. Marius steps behind me, and Rowena loops her arm through mine again. When Lady Marian moves to step aside, William grips her hand tighter and gives her a smile. Her cheeks pink and she leans into his side.

They're a good match, something I never expected to say.

William opens the door, striding inside the sitting room with his shoulders thrown back and a smile on his face.

Gasps ring out from inside. I move to follow the couple, but Rowena tugs on my arm and holds out a hand to the men behind us, and we pause in the entryway.

Rowena turns, looking up into my face. "We'll give them a few minutes to collect themselves."

We watch as William is wrapped up in the arms of his mother and sisters. Lady Marian receives a warm welcome and takes a seat on a sofa, sipping a cup of tea as she watches the reunion.

I step back from the door and take a few steps down the hallway, Rowena keeping in step with me.

When I stop, Rowena squeezes my arm. Her eyebrows are drawn together, her lips pursed and looking very kissable. "Are you okay, Alvor?"

I take a deep breath and let it out slowly. "I don't know. Will I ever be okay after learning everything my father has done? After losing my mother? I'm happy for William, that he gets to reunite with his family and have this joyful moment . . . but I can't help but wish. . ."

"I wish that, too," she whispers as she leans into my side. "You're not alone, Alvor. They're your family too. You're their nephew and cousin. You're just as welcome in that room as Red is."

My arm moves, wrapping around her waist and tugging her into an embrace. I bury my face in the curls that have come loose from her braid as I breathe in her scent. She doesn't smell like flowers, or even clean, as horse sweat clings to all of us. But underneath that, underneath the superficial, is Rowena.

"There's something to be said about the family you're born into. My mother was an angel. I don't know what my father is anymore." I shake my head. "I want what William has, Rowena. Not just the family within those walls, but the family that you have made and welcomed him into."

She leans back, eyebrows quirked. "The family I've made?"

Her eyes are hypnotizing, and I finally find the words for what I've been pondering on since I first walked into her camp. "You've made a safe haven, a family of sorts, out there in the Sherwood Forest. You have a band of merry men, who are both your brothers in arms, and makeshift father figures. At least that's what I'd assume Little John and Marius are to you. William on his own would have turned into a bitter man. Because of you, he's been loved and nurtured and welcomed into a community. I want that, because Rowena, you might think you're alone in the world, but you are far from it."

"You're not alone either, Alvor. Those people in that room are your family too. Your mother's brother stands in there, waiting for you to greet him."

"Rowena, *you* have family too."

She glares at me and I shut my mouth, not letting the rest of my words spill out. She holds my gaze for a moment before I can't resist anymore. I lean forward, brushing my lips against her forehead. She stills at my touch, and I linger for but a moment.

"You'll always have me, Rowena."

Her breath hitches. "You can't promise that, Alvor."

I lean back, smirking. "I'm a prince. I can, and I will."

Chapter Twenty-Five

A Family Most Happy

Rowena

I can't look into Alvor's eyes anymore. They're too handsome, too alluring, and the longer I'm in his embrace the more I don't want to move away.

His words patch the holes in my heart I've long ignored.

Yet, when laughter and happy voices sound closer to the door, my body finally listens and moves away from his. The loss of his warmth and comfort is immediate.

How can I be happily falling for the handsome prince in front of me while dreading the day I'll need to walk away from him? How can I be so happy for Red while yet mourning the loss of something I'll never have again?

Why are feelings so complicated, and how can I go back to the days when they were simpler?

William steps through the door, his mother's arms wrapped around his waist. "Come in, everyone, the family wants to meet you all."

We trail him into the beautiful room, an understated elegance to it that isn't present in King Ferdinand's castle. The fabrics are in rich hues, hints of gold gilding around the room in the frames and in the artwork on the walls. This is a place where I'd like to live.

Duke Scarlett approaches us first. He reaches out, pulling Alvor into a long embrace that has my throat catching. The duke finally pulls away and shakes hands with the rest of us before stopping in front of me.

The duke's blue eyes shine as he gives my hand a firm shake. "Thank you for bringing our son back to us, Rowena."

My eyebrows arch of their own volition and the duke chuckles.

"Yes, I know who you are and what you've no doubt sacrificed to save these men and my son. The kingdom thanks you. *I* thank you. If there is anything you *ever* need, do not hesitate to come to me. I will do all in my power to help you."

My throat closes, and I blink away the moisture in my eyes as I perform a perfect curtsy. "Thank you, Duke Scarlett."

He shakes his head. "No. You do not curtsy to me, Rowena. You are our family's hero. Now please sit and let us call for refreshments. We wish to hear everyone's stories and how we can assist you."

Alvor leads me over to a sofa across from which William and Lady Marian sit, his sisters flanking the two of them.

Alvor sits next to me, too much distance between us for my liking, but the perfect amount for societal propriety. Little John and Marius look around, and when Duke Scarlett gestures to empty chairs, they finally relent and seat themselves.

I can understand their hesitation. I smell like horses, and dirt coats my shoes and no doubt my clothes, yet none of the nobility in the room have batted an eye.

The duchess calls for tea and sandwiches, and before I know it, I have a dainty porcelain plate in my hand with a cucumber sandwich on top of it. Slices of meat and cheese have been placed on my plate as well as a roll, tempting me to indulge in its fluffy deliciousness.

The men have no qualms about eating, although I note that they eat with more manners than back at our camp. I pick at my meat and cheese, taking small bites, waiting for the questions to begin.

Duke Scarlett's eyes rove over the room before landing on his nephew. "Alvor, as I'm sure you're aware, your father has announced your death. The court has been sent into an upheaval. He has forbidden a mourning period and instead has announced a bridal competition." The duke's eyes flit to his daughters. "We must stop this madness."

Alvor nods, setting his plate on the small table in front of our sofa. "It's why we're here, Uncle. We have made plans. First, we should tell you that we're not sure whether my father is cursed or not."

Gasps come from the women across from us, yet Duke Scarlett seems unfazed.

Alvor clasps his hands together as he leans forward, elbows planted on his knees. "Five years ago, my father received a mirror. I cannot recall from whom, but we've determined that it's a cursed object. Somehow, my father is able to spread the darkness from the mirror to those around him. Anyone within the sound of his voice is at risk." He stops talking, turning his head to look at me. He looks at me tenderly, a soft smile on his lips. "I was under the curse's thrall until Rowena came and rescued me. My father commanded her to kill me. Instead, she hid me away, delivering the heart of a boar to him as proof of my death."

The duchess and her daughters flinch, Red's younger sister gagging before covering her mouth with a handkerchief.

Duke Scarlett sighs and rubs his chin before meeting Alvor's gaze. "After my sister died, your father was never the same. He had a good support system around him still, and I thought he'd be fine. It wasn't until . . . " He stops talking, his eyes on me, and I realize what he's trying to communicate. It wasn't until *my* father died that the king really went insane and received the cursed mirror.

I nod. "The timeline matches what we have learned for ourselves. Five years ago was when everything got worse."

The duke frowns. "When William disappeared, I withdrew from court. I couldn't stand to look at King Ferdinand after our loss. I could sense something had changed, but I could never pinpoint what."

William leans forward. "Uncle Standford explained how we can break the curse."

"You went and saw my brother before you saw me?" His mother's outrage is evident on her face.

William shrugs sheepishly. "Sorry, Mother. Rowena and Alvor needed answers, and he's the only one I know who has been to the Academy of Radiance."

Alvor clears his throat. "It was a very enlightening meeting. We know how to destroy the mirror; now it's just a matter of getting into the castle. Which is where you all come into play."

Duke Scarlett leans forward, elbows on his knees, mimicking Alvor's stance. "Tell me."

Alvor pauses, looking at me with arched eyebrows. I'm not a huge fan of pretending to go to court to be part of the bridal competition. I could just walk in as the huntress, but without a command from the king to be in the upper levels of the castle, it'd be suspicious for me to be there. Coming as a noblewoman, though, can give me an advantage, and an excuse if I were to conveniently get lost.

I nod, and Alvor turns back, explaining the plan to the group.

The Duke's eyebrows furrow. "But my daughters are his nieces? They're too closely related for your father to marry."

Alvor shakes his head. "He is not related to them by blood—I am. Thus, they fall under the umbrella of eligible young maidens."

The duchess's hand flutters to her chest, and William's sisters both look a little pale at the idea of marrying their uncle.

"That's why I will be impersonating one of your daughters," I speak up. "You've been away from court long enough that no one is familiar with their faces. I can change my hair color, wear rouge, and in a fancy dress, I can pass as a noblewoman. The king has only seen me in my hunting leathers, and often doesn't even look me in the face while talking with me. I can't say it's a foolproof plan, but it'd take someone close to me to recognize me in the finery of the aristocracy."

The duchess taps her fingers against her skirt. "But what of our neighbors and friends? Surely, they'll realize?"

I nod. "They will, *if* we draw attention to the circumstance. If we were to say, slip in at the last minute unannounced, few will notice. We only need to get into the castle that first evening. Once inside, I have a . . . special way to access the king's quarters and destroy the mirror. There's no reason for me as the huntress to be there that night, but coming as a courtier means I have an excuse for roaming the castle, lending credibility if I were to be discovered in the royal's hallway. I could claim a semblance of innocence and curiosity."

Duke Scarlett stands, pacing to the window. "One day? We only need to be there for one day?"

Alvor rises from the sofa. "Yes. Duke Scarlett, as the prince of Lyriva, I promise that we will do all in our power to destroy the mirror by the end of the night."

The duke turns slowly and walks back to Alvor. "I believe in your words, nephew. But remember who it is that will truly be fighting for our kingdom that day."

His words ring in my ears, increasing the pressure building in my head.

Me. It all relies on me.

Why does it always have to be me?

The duchess claps her hands. "Well then, if you are to attend the opening ball, we must get Rowena a new dress. The rest of you"—she turns her eyes on the men—"shall bathe. Everyone shall stay here until we're ready to travel to the capital in a few days."

My stomach drops. I haven't been back to the castle since yesterday morning. Cook needs more meat; she even said the king asked her to prepare a feast for the competition. I can't stay here and fulfill my job.

Little John clears his throat, drawing my gaze. He winks before standing and turning to the duchess. "As much as I would love to stay, I must return to camp. There are things I must take care of while the rest of you are here, so that we can avoid suspicion."

What would I do without my right-hand man?

I walk over and give the grumpy giant of a man a hug. "Thank you," I whisper. "Remember to wear your hood. I'll go hunting in two days, but Cook will need meat tomorrow."

He pats my back. "I'll take care of it."

I nod and step out of his embrace. Servants enter the room and William leaves with Lady Marian. A maid approaches me and curtsies. "This way, my lady."

I shake my head. "Oh, I'm not—"

Alvor glares at me, as if daring me to finish the sentence. I stare right back. The sudden urge to stick my tongue out at him strikes me. I really need to break the ridiculous notion that I'm anywhere close to being a lady. Alvor stares back, arching his eyebrows at me after a long moment. I roll my eyes and huff.

Fine. If he wants a lady, then a lady is what he'll get.

Chapter Twenty-Six

A Discussion Most Long

Alvor

I haven't seen Rowena since we retired for the evening yesterday—a situation I need to remedy this morning. My boots echo on the stone hallway as I weave through the castle, passing servants and windows until I finally spot her through a windowpane.

She's with Lady Marian in the gardens. This is perfect. I can take her on a romantic walk through the flowers, and I'm sure I can find William somewhere so he can walk with Lady Marian.

I turn, ready to go hunt down my errant cousin, and instead am greeted by my uncle's serious face. "Alvor, I'm glad I found you. I hope you slept well."

I nod. "I did. Better than I've slept in a while."

My eyes flick toward the window again, and my uncle notices. He chuckles. "Before you go out and speak with the young ladies, I'd like to talk with you in my study."

My heart sinks. I'm not ready to face the hardship before us quite yet. But I can't deny my uncle's request after his generous hospitality.

"Lead the way."

He claps me on the shoulder before turning and heading down the hallway. I trail behind him, leaving my heart behind in the gardens.

He leads me to a room deep in the heart of the castle. When he opens the door, the scent of paper and ink reaches my nose. Books line the walls, and my uncle's desk is overflowing with papers. I take a seat across the desk from him and lean back in the leather chair.

He sits, folding his hands. "Alvor, the kingdom is in crisis."

I nod. "I've become aware."

My uncle frowns. "It's more than just your father, Alvor. I might not attend court functions, but I keep my ear to the ground, and there are rumors that Rovia wants to attack us. They complain of poor crops being traded and merchants being imprisoned for not giving your father what he wants. With the throne so unstable, we risk being overtaken by Rovia or Uxia if we don't do something strategic to change our standing amongst the kingdoms. It's been years since there's been war between the kingdoms of Miraveil, but I'm afraid if nothing changes, the peace will be destroyed."

I steeple my fingers on the desk, leaning the tips of them against my chin. "What would you advise?"

He rubs his chin. "As much as I hate the idea, a political marriage of convenience would be wise. If we could ally ourselves with Rovia or Uxia, it would go a long way in strengthening our borders and showing stability."

I shake my head. "No. I'm willing to marry, but I will only marry for love."

My uncle quirks a brow. "Don't think I missed how you watched Rowena. You know that won't work out between you, Alvor. She's a huntress. Her father was a commoner, even if he was friends with the king."

There's more to Rowena's family history than just her father. I tilt my head, studying my uncle. How easily he has forgotten about his sister and her closest friend. Granted, we lost them ten years ago—but still. We are more than just the patriarchal side of our family.

At least, I hope I am.

I really don't want to be like my father.

For once, I wish I had magic, that my mother's side would have given me something. But Red gets his talents from his mother, not his father who sits before me.

But Rowena isn't sharing her secret, and so neither will I, though it might solve these issues I seem to be facing. "Uncle, I understand your concerns. But wouldn't it be better for our kingdom if I were to marry a woman from our own lands? A commoner, as you so put it? Wouldn't that rally the people around me? They'd feel like they have someone to represent them, a voice in the matter, an advocate in the running of the kingdom. If we survive this adventure, then Rowena will be my choice."

My uncle leans back in his chair, stroking his beard. "You love her?"

After the past few days, and my memories of our time together as children, I no longer have an ounce of doubt. "I have for a long time." I pause, spearing my uncle with my gaze. "Let me be clear: I would rather die before I marry anyone else, Uncle."

His eyebrows arch and he chuckles. "That's it, then. Now, how do we keep our lands stable without a marriage contract?"

I lean closer. "I have a few ideas."

"Please." He gestures as if I were taking the stage. I guess I am, seeing as I need to present all the thoughts that have been running through my head over the past few days.

We talk about crops, the military, trade agreements, taxes, and so many other topics, exchanging ideas and studying books of history when needed. Our discussion is only interrupted when a servant comes to bring us to supper.

Regret slithers through me that I haven't spent any time with Rowena yet today, but it's contrasted by how much better I feel after talking to my uncle about the future and taking the throne.

I trail my uncle to the dining hall. When we enter the room, my gaze is drawn instantly to one woman.

Rowena is beautiful, whether she's wearing her hunting leathers or a peasant's gown; it's not the clothing that makes her attractive—it's the light glowing from within her.

But I cannot deny that seeing her in an elaborate gown, her hair curled and pinned atop her head, with a hint of rouge on her cheeks, takes my breath away.

She glides over to me, her steps measured and dainty compared to her normal powerful stride. She pulls a fan from her pocket, flicking it open, and waving it at her face coyly. "Prince Alvor, it seems you've yet to ready for the evening meal?"

I bow low before straightening and catching her hand that holds the fan, stilling the motion. I clasp her fingers, bringing them to my lips, where I place a kiss on each knuckle. "How could I spend a second more away from you, my lady? It has been exquisite torture not spending every minute of the day in your presence, something I wish to remedy immediately."

There's a snort from behind me. "You two are disgustingly sweet," William says as he tugs on my arm, pulling me back toward the hallway. "Mother says you need to change after spending all day with Father. We'll hold off on the meal until you're ready."

Rowena pulls her hand out of mine, flicking her fan open across her face again.

I want to rip the thing away immediately because it's blocking her smile.

"Shall we resume this enchanting charade in a few moments?" Her eyelashes flutter, and I can't help it. I laugh.

Then, I'm not the only one, and Rowena has dissolved into a fit of giggles beside me while Red chuckles.

Rowena swipes a tear from her cheeks. "Oh, I'm glad that's over with. I couldn't keep that up much longer."

I chuckle. "Keep acting like that and no one will recognize you at my father's castle."

She wiggles her eyebrows, a playfulness I haven't seen from her in years. "So it was working?"

My gaze drops from her eyes to her lips, a sudden hunger growing within me. "Yes, it was *definitely* working."

William groans from beside me. "Stop flirting, you two. Now Alvor, go change for supper. Mother wants us all in our finery. She said to borrow my clothes until the tailor arrives tomorrow."

I don't respond. Honestly, I can't. Because Rowena's gaze has dropped to the vicinity of my lips, and I'm positive I'm not the only one feeling the tug between us to move closer.

That is, until I'm yanked away by my cousin.

"Flirt later. Food now," William grinds out as he tugs me toward the hallway.

Rowena smiles and then uses that confounded fan again, though this time it might truly be to cool the blush flaming her cheeks.

Chapter Twenty-Seven

A Sheriff Most Despicable

Rowena

A branch snaps underfoot, and I go still. My magic unfurls, and I take a relieved breath when the only living things around me are the small animals of the forest.

I need to focus.

But how am I supposed to focus after sleeping two nights in a feathered mattress in a castle, where the food is more delicious than I can imagine and where they have dessert? It's been five years since I've had a real dessert. I mean, I've occasionally been able to filch a pastry from Cook, but it's been too long since I've indulged in chocolate pudding.

I can't untaste it; the flavor haunts my dreams.

I'm distracted again when my magic flares within me.

There's a goose ahead, near a pond, and it's in pain. I pull an arrow from my quiver.

Luckily, Little John let me pack my things before we left camp. It meant I could travel from Duke Scarlett's castle to the edge of Sherwood Forest closest to the capital without stopping at camp.

I shove all thoughts aside as I make my way through the underbrush. There, several yards away, is a goose honking. The poor animal's wing is bent at an unnatural angle.

My arrow flies, ending the poor creature's suffering and my search for something to bring to Cook.

The rest of the trip back to the castle goes smoothly. I'm blessed with finding a few more fowl, a rich bounty that should last for a day or two if Cook handles the meat right.

When I slip into the kitchen I'm greeted by chaos. Double the amount of undercooks are around, and maids are weaving through the masses, arms full with heaps of laundry and cleaning supplies.

I weave through the crowd until I see Cook's silver-tinted hair at the center of everything, her strong voice barking out orders to anyone within earshot.

When she sees me, her eyes widen, nostrils flaring before she glares. "Drop the goose and get out."

My eyebrows lower. "I have news."

Cook huffs. "I don't have time for your news. The king is in a tizzy, and I already have too many people to deal with. I'm in charge of cooking a feast for all the noblemen and women in the kingdom in two days, girl. So drop the goose and go find me a hundred more."

A hundred more?

Cook rolls her eyes. "Not a hundred. But I need you to bring me more than what you've got. Your replacement brought me a good amount yesterday, but I'll need the two of you to work together to bring me enough for the feast."

My heart seizes in my chest. I can't spend the next two days hunting. I need to be planning with Alvor. I need to be . . . not suspicious.

If I'm hunting, then the king won't realize I'll have time to be deceiving him by meeting with Duke Scarlett.

A plan forms in my mind. Little John can hunt for me, along with Much and Stue, while Dale runs the camp. I'll do what I can today, but I'm meeting with the seamstress tomorrow, and I can't miss that without incurring the duchess's wrath and putting our plans in danger.

I take the goose over to the dressing table and hand it to a young girl before approaching Cook. "I decided to take on an apprentice. He'll deliver the meat."

Her eyebrows arch. "Good. About time you got an apprentice. Now grab an apple turnover and be on your way."

I smirk. "One turnover, or two?"

Cook's lips purse. "Two, and only because I'm feeling generous today. But you better share the other one."

I pat the woman's shoulder before grabbing two pastries from a basket and making a quick exit from the craziness.

I slip into the forest, traveling around the edge of Nottingham as I head toward Little John's favorite section of the forest to hunt in.

A shout breaks through my concentration, and my running feet slow. A woman's voice rings out across the clearing to my right. I turn, racing into the open area only to see a little boy running full tilt toward me. A woman stands farther away, blocking the way of a burly man with a beard I frustratingly recognize.

The sheriff of Nottingham, chief tax collector, and a man who doesn't need to be cursed to be evil.

"Run, Caleb!" the woman shouts, and when the little boy sees me, he only slows for a fraction of a second before veering to the left so we don't collide.

I hold out my hands. "You don't need to fear me."

He slows, glancing back for a moment before frowning. "Momma said to run. I need to find Robin Hood. That's what the nice man said."

I tilt my head, glancing back at the woman and Sheriff for a moment before focusing on Caleb. "Nice man?"

Caleb opens his hand, a silver coin in his palm. "He gave us this money so we could eat. But the sheriff . . . somehow he discovered we all had more coins. He's been taking them away. Momma said to run."

My blood boils and I reach out, gripping the little boy's hand. "Your momma is right. Run into the forest, search the ground for a deer trail. When you find it, follow it, eventually it'll lead you to Robin Hood's camp. But you have to look very carefully; the deer trails are hard to find."

"Yes'm," he says before scurrying off into the forest.

I notch an arrow in my bow, but keep it pointed at the ground. I stop ten feet from the woman and Sheriff. "What's going on here?"

The sheriff, who probably has a real name but I hate him too much to want to use it, sneers at me. "Nothing that concerns you, huntress. Go back to gathering rabbits for the king. Some of us have real business to attend to."

I scoff. "As if me putting meat on the king's table isn't real business. Now what are you doing bothering this poor woman?"

Said woman takes a step back and toward me, but then the sheriff grabs her arm tightly.

Not on my watch.

I pull my arrow back, aiming at his heart. "Let her go."

He snarls. "If you shoot me, you're a dead woman walking."

My eyebrows arch. "If I shoot you, you'll be dead. So I don't think you can really say what I'll be after that."

He lets the woman go, shoving her away from him. "She owes taxes, and somehow got a few extra coins recently. I came to collect them, but she wouldn't hand them over. So we're having a little discussion about the consequences of not paying the king's tax."

I lower my bow once the woman is behind me, and aim for his thigh instead of his heart. "Which are?"

He smirks. "Well, she could have handed over the coins or . . . negotiated with me."

The woman spits on the ground. "I will never give you what you want. I'd rather die."

The sheriff's grin is as dark as the king's. "That could be arranged."

A wound to the thigh isn't enough for this man, and I move it back up to aim for his heart. "No one will be dying today or paying any such taxes."

The sheriff draws a dagger from his waistband. "You don't get to decide that, huntress. Step aside."

I shake my head. "Never. I will not let you hurt innocent women and children for the king."

He stalks toward me. "Too late for that. Now step aside."

"No."

My arrow releases, my muscles quaking from having had the bow drawn for so long. It flies wide, and before I'm able to pull another one, the sheriff swipes at me with his dagger.

I move to the side, the tip grazing my leather jerkin.

The woman is already on the move, running toward the forest where her son disappeared.

Meanwhile, my gaze is firmly fixed on the bearded man stalking me with death written across his face.

"Little girls like you need to learn to listen to those in charge," he growls as he slices his dagger through the air, aiming for my chest. I block it with my bow, the knife cutting into the precious wood.

I grunt as I push against his arm. "Ugly men like you need to learn that us women are more powerful than you think."

My ankle hooks around his, and I yank his leg out from underneath him. His eyes go wide, and just as confidence floods through me, a sharp pain in my arm catches my attention.

The dagger I took my eyes off of has sliced through my sleeve and into my arm.

The sheriff lands on his back and quickly rolls over, assuming a fighting position.

It's too late, though, because, despite the injury, his fall allowed me enough time to hook my bow on my back and pull the daggers from my thigh holsters.

I clamp my mouth closed, holding in the words I know would only anger him. There is no time for me to antagonize the disgusting man. He drew first blood, and who knows when the last time he cleaned his dagger was. I need to get this treated and fast.

The sheriff snarls and lunges for me. This time I'm prepared. Little John's fighting lessons kick in, and I move with the fluidity of years of practice and daily exercise.

The dodge comes naturally, as does the kick to his knee. He grunts, spinning to face me, and I take the opportunity to slice his arm in the same place he got mine. He yells out, but I stay silent, eyes narrowed, watching his every move.

He snarls. "You think that's going to intimidate me?"

My answer comes in the form of another wound to his opposite arm.

"Intimidated yet?" The words slip out of my mouth, and I know Little John would be shaking his head at me. Silence intimidates more than words is what he always says—or rather doesn't say.

What little amount of the sheriff's face that isn't covered in hair is mottled red. "You're dead, little huntress."

"You'll have to catch me first."

I run as fast as I've ever run in my life into the forest. I head north, opposite of our camp.

It's as if a wild boar is chasing me for all of the growling and huffing and puffing sounding from behind me. Despite my injury that burns like fire,

I race through the undergrowth, experience leading me as I do my best to imitate a white-tailed deer's swift fleeing abilities.

Sweat drips down my brow, and my head pounds in time with the pulsating pain of the cut on my arm. Tree branches whip across my face, and bush thorns snag on my sleeves as I plunge into the thickest portions of the forest.

Soon the only sounds I hear are my pounding feet and ragged breathing, the sheriff's footfalls having fallen behind me. I slow down, but at this point, I'm in a portion of the forest I'm unfamiliar with. I could be close to the Rovia border if I cut northwest through the forest, far away from Duke Scarlett's estates.

I pause, leaning against a tree, and take the moment to inspect my arm. My sleeve is soaked in blood, and when my head spins, I'm not surprised. I slide down the bark and reach down, tearing a portion of my undershirt. I loop the fabric around the cut and, with my teeth, tighten the knot.

I blink away the hot tears and stare up into the canopy. The sky has darkened beyond the leaves.

My breathing slows back to its normal rhythm as I try and get my mind to create a plan.

But I can't.

All I've got is the knowledge that I need to get my wound treated, and I need to get out of this forest.

Except, I'm afraid the darkness is closing in, and neither one of those things will happen tonight.

Chapter Twenty-Eight

A Prince Most Worried

Alvor

I slam my fist against William's door, pounding on it before throwing it open. His startled face greets me a foot from the entryway.

"Alvor, what's wrong?"

"Rowena isn't back yet, and nobody has seen her since this morning."

William shrugs as if this is no big deal, when, in fact, it *is* a big deal. "She's probably out hunting."

I start pacing. "The evening meal has passed and the sun has set. She said she'd be back tonight, and she is not here. Something is wrong, William."

"Calm down, Alvor. She knows how to handle herself."

I shake my head, the panic in my chest rising with each moment. "No. I can feel it. Something is wrong. We need to find her."

He rolls his eyes and leans back against the wall, watching me wear a trail in the ornamental rug on the floor. "Let's wait until morning. If she's not back then, we'll send Marius back to camp to see if she's there."

My fingers find my hair, running through it and tugging at the ends. "We should have sent someone with her. We should have made a better plan. She's the key to this, cousin. If we lose her, we lose everything."

"Alvor, Robin is a skilled hunter. She knows the woods better than anybody. She's careful, and she's talented. She knows how to take care of herself."

"Yes, but who takes care of her, William? She's not a rock. She's a human with needs. Who has been taking care of her? Who worries over her? Clearly, it's not you."

"You think I don't worry about her? I've spent the past three years befriending her, Alvor. I've lived in her camp, seen her almost every day, while you didn't even remember to talk to her for five years. So don't tell me that I don't care."

His words cut through my anger, and I slump down into a chair by the fireplace. I bury my face in my hands. "I'm sorry. I just . . . I'm worried, and I don't know what to do about it."

"I understand you're worried, but you can't take it out on others when you feel something uncomfortable, cousin."

My stomach twists as I realize just how like my father I was these last few moments. The words of superiority unfitting for the situation and who I was speaking with. I clench my jaw and rub my eyes, swallowing the lump in my throat as my belly roils.

"I'm sorry," I whisper.

A warm hand lands on my shoulder. "You're forgiven. Now, why don't we ride out and see if we can find Robin? If you're this worried about her, then I doubt I'll get a wink of sleep tonight."

I raise my head and meet his gaze. "Are you sure?"

He nods. "If we're out all night, at least maybe that will give us an excuse to not meet with the tailors tomorrow. Mother is insistent on a new wardrobe, but I'd rather hide in the forest than get fancy new clothes."

I raise my eyebrows. "But what does Lady Marian think about you getting a new wardrobe?"

William sighs. "To be honest, she was a tad disappointed when I got rid of the highwayman mask, though I think she'll still have me even if my name comes with a title."

I stand up, slapping his shoulder in kind. "Then it must be true love."

My cousin smirks, and we exit his room quickly, heading toward the stables. Just as we're saddling our horses, Little John rides into the courtyard. He dismounts and rushes toward us. "Have you seen Robin?"

My chest seizes at his question, my mind racing with worries. "No. What's wrong?"

He frowns. "Cook said she went hunting. That we were supposed to bring in as many fowl as we could today. Except, Robin never told me that. Then the little boy from Nottingham made it to camp with his mother, said Robin fought off the sheriff to protect them."

I spit out my next words through clenched teeth. "The Sheriff of Nottingham?"

Little John nods, his face drawn.

William's voice is hollow. "You were right, Alvor. She is in trouble."

I stare down Little John. "Let's work our way from here back to where she fought the sheriff. See if we can't find her. Maybe she was on her way here and you missed her."

Little John winces. "She's injured. The mother stayed long enough to watch the fight and saw the sheriff cut her arm. I'm . . . I'm afraid, Alvor. If she's injured, that complicates things."

"I'll get my uncle," William murmurs and mounts his horse, riding away without another word.

I rub my forehead, the ache from my heart spreading to my brain. "If she was running away from him, she would have led him away from camp. Let's search the forest closest to Rovia."

Little John is a man of few words, and I'm grateful he doesn't offer platitudes as we mount up and head out of the stables. I leave a brief message with the stable master for the duke. He has us wait a moment before returning with lanterns and extra vessels of oil that we store in our saddlebags.

We exit the gates and head toward the forest. Little John leads me into the undergrowth, but it's not long before I call out to him to stop.

He quirks his eyebrows, but I hold up my hand.

The worry from earlier has abated, but now there's a tugging sensation in my chest, as if there's a thread tied to my heart and it's pulling me toward something . . . or someone.

"I think we're going the wrong way." I twist in my saddle until it feels as if I'm being pulled straight forward. "This way."

I turn my horse and lead out, Little John falling behind me. Every few moments, I adjust our direction, trusting in this foreign sensation to guide us.

I can't help it. It feels like Rowena's light. Memories of the moments of lucidity in my father's presence, the night I cried in her lap as her magic brought light to the room, all are wrapped around this simple thread tugging me deeper into the forest.

The canopy overhead thickens, and I slow our pace, holding the lantern up as much as possible to help guide my horse around the many obstacles in our path.

The string tightens, as if turning into a thicker piece of yarn, incessantly pulling forward and to my right.

I can't stand it anymore. I dismount, pulling the reins over my mount's head so I can lead him forward as I jog in the direction this mysterious magic is guiding me toward.

The lantern light catches on movement, eyes flashing in the dark, and as I draw closer, I see that it's not just one pair of eyes. It's many.

Squirrels, deer, and even a fox scatter as I enter a small clearing. As I walk farther into the grass, I see the figure they were surrounding, and another pair of eyes meets mine.

The doe looks at me for a moment before turning and nudging Rowena's cheeks with her nose. Rowena, whose head rests against the doe's back, slumbers on, her body reposed as if she's in the most comfortable bed. As I approach, I see a small light emanating from her hand. Just a single fingertip glows, and from it a small wisp of light cuts through the night, fading away into the darkness. But the light? Well . . . it's clearly pointing toward me.

My steps are slow, and I lower myself to my knees in front of the doe who moves to block Rowena's face with her body.

"It's alright," I whisper. "I've come to help her, as you have done."

The doe inclines her head before moving and allowing me access to Rowena. I take my time, inspecting her wrapped arm. The wound has stopped bleeding. I can't find any others, and so I slip my arm beneath her head, my hand brushing against the doe's hide. When I lift her, the deer scrambles to her feet and flees back into the forest.

Rowena doesn't wake, but when I tuck her hand against my chest, the light flares before winking out. Peace fills my soul. Somehow her gift, that great gift from Solwain, has protected her again. I'll have to ask her more about it in the future. For now, I place another kiss on her hair and savor the feel of her in my arms.

Little John approaches, and between the two of us, I'm able to mount my horse again and hold Rowena against me as we head back to my uncle's castle.

The entire time I breathe her in, soaking up every second of holding her in my arms and breathing in her earthy scent that's tinged with iron.

As we ride into the courtyard a cry goes out. William, with Standford right behind him, greets us as we enter the stables.

"Is she okay?" William asks as I hand Rowena down from atop my horse. He cradles her in his arms and grumbles, "Of course she's not okay, she's unconscious in my arms. Uncle, you must do something!"

Standford frowns and shakes his head ruefully. "Carry her inside. I'm not examining her in the stables, nephew."

I hand my reins to a stable boy and trail them inside, Little John right behind me.

William carries Rowena to a guest room off the main hallway, and after securing her on a bed, rings for a servant.

Standford moves to the right side of the bed while I take up vigil opposite him. He places his hands on her head, light flowing from them into her body. "Cut on her arm; it's deep and will require stitches. She's had a good deal of blood loss, and her magic is oddly drained. She must have used a lot of it today."

"Her magic led me to her, Standford. I don't know how, but I could feel where she was, as if it was drawing me to her."

Standford's blue eyes widen. "I've never heard of it doing such a thing."

I shrug. "I know what I felt, Doctor."

He nods. "I'm not questioning you, my prince. The magic from Solwain is mysterious. In some ways it's predictable; in others it chooses to be creative. I'm only surprised and curious, not doubting."

I tilt my head, watching Rowena's face relax as Standford's magic does its work. "Why is it so different for everyone? Why is the magic not just one thing done one way?"

"Why is each person in the world so different from the other? Yet also, so similar? There are basic rules of magic, such as using it for good, and that it's based on light. But then I think Solwain lets us each have something unique that somehow will bless us and the lives of others. There are families who have healing magic, but it works differently for each person. Some have animal, plant, or water magic. But each person's abilities are unique."

I mull over his words, and somehow I have more questions than when I started. When Rowena sighs, a contented sound, I shove them all away. I kneel down, reaching for her hand and gripping it. "What is your magic doing right now?"

He grins. “Taking away the pain. I’ll need to stitch her cut closed, and I don’t want her to feel it. I’m numbing the site. I’m also trying to replenish her blood supply, urge her body to make more and faster. Sometimes that works.”

“Sometimes?”

He quirks a brow. “Were you not just listening to my magic lesson, young prince? Solwain is in charge of magic and our lives. Sometimes things aren’t meant to be changed because of the plan Solwain has for us. But I imagine we’ll need this young lady for many years to come with the way you’re looking at her, so I hope he’ll allow my magic to help urge her body to heal faster.”

I shake my head. “I don’t understand it all.”

Standford chuckles. “It takes a lifetime of study, Prince Alvor. For now, just have faith.”

Rowena sighs again, her head tilting toward me. Standford removes his hands just as a servant comes into the room holding rags and hot water. “Perfect, bring those over here.”

I bury my head in the sheets, unable to stomach the sight of the wound. I grip Rowena’s hands as Standford stitches up the cut on her arm.

When he finishes, Marian enters the room, my aunt trailing behind her.

“Oh good,” Marian says. “She’s all stitched up. That means all of you men can leave and let us women care for her.” She playfully pushes William toward the door, but I don’t move. Her eyes find mine. “Prince Alvor, I know you’re in love with her, but a lady needs her privacy if she’s going to be changed out of her hunting gear, don’t you think? I doubt Robin Hood would want a bunch of men to see her in her underthings.”

My eyebrows arch. "You know?"

She rolls her eyes. "Of course I do. You should know better than to underestimate a woman's observation skills by now. So stop it."

I bow my head. "I apologize."

Marian waves a hand in the air as if brushing away my words. "Apology accepted. Now, out."

I squeeze Rowena's hand one last time, placing a kiss on her knuckles, before standing. I walk to the door but pause before exiting. "Take good care of her?"

Marian smiles. "She's our future queen. Of course we will."

Then she slams the door in my face.

Chapter Twenty-Nine

A Dress Most Delightful

Rowena

A warm hand squeezes mine, pulling me from a blissful dream of sleeping on a feathered mattress instead of the hard ground where I fell unconscious.

It was such a nice dream—but this hand keeps squeezing mine.

Why is it doing that?

I force my eyes open, though they're scratchy and dry, as if I slept for hours.

"Rowena?"

I can hear Alvor's voice, but that's not right. I'm out in the forest; why is he here?

"Rowena, can you hear me?"

I lick my lips and turn my head, trying to form words as I process what I'm seeing. "Alvor?"

He grins, his dark hair flopping across his forehead. "I'm glad you're finally awake."

My nose scrunches. "What do you mean, finally?"

His thumb runs over my knuckles, temporarily distracting me. But when he starts speaking, I refocus on his lips.

They look very kissable.

Wow, I must be out of it.

Maybe not a lot, because I've been thinking about kissing Alvor a lot lately.

But like, wow, with him clean shaven, those lips look extra nice.

"Rowena, are you listening to me?" Alvor's smirking. He just said something. Wait, what did he just say?

"Huh?" I mumble.

"Rowena, you've been asleep for a day and a half."

I sit up straight in bed, clutching the blanket to my chest. "What?!"

Alvor leans back in the chair next to my bedside. "When we brought you back from the forest, you were unconscious. Standford worked to heal you, but as part of that it seems you decided to sleep for thirty-six hours."

I slap his shoulder. "And you just let me? Alvor, we have things to do! We're so behind!"

He shrugs. "No, we're not. You needed your sleep, and the rest of us have everything handled."

My hand goes up to my loose hair, weaving into the messy curls, as my mind finally decides to wake up and focus. "What about Cook? I was supposed to do two days of hunting."

He draws a check in the air. "Little John and Stue took care of that. Though I don't think those two will be hunting together again anytime soon."

I shiver. "Stue sneezes and scares off the game . . ." I trail off, my mind already racing to the next thought. "Wait. We're supposed to go to the capital today."

He nods, looking all calm and peaceful—the complete opposite of how I'm feeling right now. "Everything is packed and ready. We're just waiting for you. Standford told us once you woke to feed you a large meal, and then you should be fine."

My stomach, ever on cue, chooses that moment to make itself known with a noise that makes me want to bury my head under the covers.

"I'm guessing you want that food now?"

I peek through the curtain of hair currently hiding my face so that I can glare at the handsome prince. "Yes." Then, I grab a pillow from behind me and hit him across the face with it.

He gapes at me, and there's a tittering from the door.

It's only then I realize we're not alone in the room together.

A maid covers her mouth, her eyes crinkled with laughter.

This time, I really hide beneath the blankets, and the only sign that Alvor leaves is that his laughter trails out of the room behind him.

I'm blaming the empty stomach for my rationale. Because only that could convince me that hitting a handsome prince in the face with a pillow is a much better idea than kissing him senseless.

The plate of food before me has been utterly demolished. I've never been so hungry in my life. When the maid told me Doctor Standford said it was my wound and magical depletion, I believed it.

But now I feel better than ever. Maybe Dale helped prepare my food or something, because I'm positively brimming with energy.

There's a thin line of stitches on my arm, but it doesn't hurt, and it looks as if it's a week-old wound instead of two days old.

I'm grateful the maid helped me slip into this long-sleeved dress. Its puffy sleeves give my arms room to breathe, and though I personally find the style unbecoming, I know I'll fit right in at court.

There's a knock on the door, and the maid opens it, letting in Alvor. She curtsies before leaving the door open and retreating down the hallway.

Ah yes, rules of propriety. Somehow, those don't seem to exist in the forest.

Alvor saunters into the room in the hunting leathers of the merry men, not the starched white shirt and collared jacket of a prince.

I can't decide which look I like better.

"You're beautiful," he whispers as he stops in front of me. He holds out his hands, and I slip my fingers into his. He tightens his grip, tugging me closer as if he wants to pull me into an embrace. Except there's a hoop skirt and layers of fabric acting as a barrier between us.

I step back, frowning. "Alvor, the dress. I don't dare get an ounce of dirt on this thing. It costs enough to feed a family for a month, you know."

He smirks and lifts my hands to his lips. "I know," he whispers before placing a kiss on the back of one hand and then the other.

"Alvor, are you sure about this? I don't know how I feel about you being in the castle the whole time. What if your father finds you?"

He flips my right hand over, lips trailing to my palm and then my inner wrist before he pauses. "That's why you're making me a map of the hidden passageways, remember? You can't really expect me to stand by while you make all the sacrifices for my kingdom. You may not see me, but I'll be holding you up, supporting you where you stand, and preventing anyone from thwarting our plans."

I shake my head. "If I can't see you, then you can't support me where I stand, princeling."

He frowns. "I thought I had gotten rid of the nickname."

I shrug. "Not when you say ridiculous things."

His blue eyes spark, and his hands drop mine, coming up and cradling my face in his calloused palms. "Rowena de Frossard, I love you. I will not abandon you in the hour when you save my people. *Our* people. I will guard your back with my sword. I will be there in the shadows, waiting to steady you when you waver. Nothing will keep me away from standing beside you in the light or in the dark."

Alvor's face blurs, and his thumb strokes my cheekbone, wiping away the stray tear that's probably smeared the rouge the maid put on my cheeks.

"Alvor," I breathe. "The kingdom will be nothing without you."

He shakes his head, leaning his forehead down against mine, pushing the hoops of my skirts backward so he can close the distance between us. "Wrong. The kingdom will survive. We all will. But I would be *nothing* without you, and I will not let you go into my father's castle without being there in the shadows. You're worth the risk." He leans down, tilting my face upward until his nose brushes mine. "You're my everything, Rowena de Frossard, and I cannot wait until I get to tell everyone who you really are."

"Alvor ..."

"Yes?" His lips brush against mine. It's the faintest sensation, but one that unleashes a million butterflies in my stomach.

"Do you mean it?"

He huffs a laugh as he pulls back, looking into my eyes. "Let me show you."

My eyebrows pull together, but as his face draws closer to mine, my eyes close and I'm enveloped in Alvor. He smells of pine trees, dirt, the young boy I first had a crush on, and the man I've fallen in love with. His touch is gentle as his lips caress mine. His hands cradle my face, and I reach up, gripping his forearms as he tells me just how much he cares for me.

This kiss is everything I've wanted since I was old enough to want Alvor. Those daydreams of a young, tender girl could never compare to being loved by Alvor as a woman. He makes me feel strong, and yet I know I can be weak when I'm with him.

His lips move against mine, slow and steady. With every brush, my heart pounds, the fire inside me burning brighter until I'm the one reaching up for him. My hand comes up to his face, brushing the smooth skin of his shaven face before entwining in his silky, smooth hair.

A shiver runs through my body as he deepens the kiss for a moment. Then, he pulls back. I keep my eyes closed, hoping he just needed to breathe. Instead of coming back to my mouth, his lips move to my cheek, trailing tingle-inducing kisses along my skin, until he whispers in my ear, "Rowena, you have no idea how long I've been waiting to kiss you."

That's enough distance between us, thank you very much. I tilt his head, brushing my lips against his with a contented sigh. "Since we had the archery tournament against each other when I was thirteen?"

He chuckles, nipping my bottom lip and sending my stomach swooping with butterflies. "How did you know?"

My hands move from his hair to his collar as I lean back until I can look into his eyes. "I've wanted to kiss you for just as long."

The sky-blue color of his irises darkens to a rich sapphire hue. He pauses for only a moment before his lips meet mine in an urgent exchange.

Silk dresses and propriety be hanged. Alvor pulls me against his chest in a tight embrace, kissing me with the feelings we've been holding in for most of our lives.

A whistle breaks through the haze of love and kisses, bringing me sharply back to reality.

"Cousin," Red drawls from where he leans against the door frame of my room. "You weren't supposed to kiss her until *after* we succeed."

Alvor pulls back, resting his forehead against mine. "William Scarlett. If you do not leave *immediately*, I will strip you of an inheritance."

Red scoffs. "Like I need one. Just came to say that father is waiting for Robin." He pauses, looking me over from head to toe. "But I best tell him she's running late and her maid was putting the finishing touches on her hair. I'm of a particular mind to mention that a certain prince ruined her hair in the first place."

My cheeks burn and I pull away. Alvor frowns at the separation. I pat my hair only to find two locks that have fallen out of the elaborate style. But I can't bring myself to care.

"William," Alvor growls, his eyes still on my face.

I glance at Red, who is inspecting his fingernails. "Not leaving, cousin. It seems the two of you require a chaperone."

Alvor pinches the bridge of his nose, and the motion is so adorable that I can't help but giggle.

I pop up on my toes and kiss Alvor on the cheek, tugging him down until I can whisper in his ear. "I love you, too. When we've won, you can kiss me again."

Alvor smirks. "I'm holding you to that."

"I'm counting on it."

He lets go of my waist and walks backward toward the door. "We're not done talking about that little tidbit you told me either. I want to know everything."

I shake my head, shooing him out the door. "Such a demanding prince."

Alvor winks, a motion entirely too attractive, and then turns to walk down the hallway.

Red stands up straight, a crooked grin on his face. "I'm happy for you, Robin. You're a good match."

"I agree."

Chapter Thirty

A Hallway Most Dark

Alvor

I crave Rowena's touch the minute I leave her room. The feel of her lips on mine haunts me as we ride across the kingdom into the evening. The scent of her hair, having been washed and styled, reminded me of the lilacs that bloom each spring as the sun starts its descent.

We approach the castle walls, and I pull my hood lower over my brow. Little John does the same before leading the way through the gate and into the castle gardens.

The smell of roasted pheasant reminds me of the night Rowena broke my curse, and the smell grows stronger as we slip into the kitchen. Her lips have branded me, her love seared my heart, and I can never go back to a life without her in it.

We deposit the birds Little John shot earlier on the dressing table. Cook spares us a glance, her gray eyes catching on mine for but a second. She pauses her instructions to one of the undercooks and points at us. "You two, grab an apple turnover for yourselves on your way out. Thank you for the birds."

Gratitude? An odd thing for Cook to say, but I won't deny myself of her pastries.

I take one from the basket on the counter and walk toward the edge of the kitchen, trying to blend in with the walls. Little John nods and heads back out into the forest, his hand empty. He'll meet with the rest of the men as I stay among the hidden walkways. They're to come check on me and Rowena if I don't report back in tomorrow morning.

I lean against the wall, nibbling the pastry. Its cinnamon flavor tastes like home, though there's an odd aftertaste to this one. It's almost as if it got burnt, or cooked too long, but just a fraction of a second more than normal.

I shove the rest of it in my mouth and slip around the corner. I keep my steps as silent as I can as I head up the servant stairs. A familiar hallway greets me, and I turn into the gallery, brushing my fingers against our mothers' portraits before slipping into the hidden hallway.

Seriously, how did I not find these as a boy?

I'm blaming prince duties and a certain secretive huntress.

Pinpricks of light come in through spy holes in the walls, lighting my way as I follow the map Rowena made. The noise of the welcoming ball greets me before I make it to the hallway I'm looking for. I stuff my ears with the waxed cotton William and I made earlier as I peer into the ballroom. This wall is behind the throne, which is raised high above the rest of the room where my father can lord over the proceedings.

The murmurs of the finely dressed crowd filter through my earplugs until things go quiet. I can't make out my father's words, but I recognize his tone.

It becomes harder to breathe the longer I listen to the murmurs of his voice. My stomach twists, even as my muscles tense. My teeth ache from how tightly I clench my jaw.

I force myself back to the peephole, watching everyone else but the man I've lost all respect for—curse or no curse.

It's then that I see her. The crowd turns to the doors, parting as Rowena walks down the steps to the ballroom floor on my uncle's arm.

No woman has looked more like a queen than Rowena in this moment. Her progress is slow as she crosses the room, and I drink her in. The makeup, the dress, her towering hair, which she added a wig to, all disguise her natural beauty by enhancing it and turning her into someone different. I know it's her, but it's the perfect disguise, for no one else will recognize my huntress among her finery.

She curtsies to my father; my uncle bows low.

The urge to unplug my ears is so strong, but I resist. My father's poison can't take hold of me again.

Jealousy rears its ugly head as the music begins, and a young merchant's son, whose gaze lingers on Rowena's form, approaches her with a smarmy smile. I've seen enough, and I don't know if my stomach can handle any more of this.

I step back from the wall and pull out the map again. I can't stay here watching Rowena dance the night away. I need something to do, to feel productive and like I'm contributing to this plan.

My eyes alight on the royal wing and the path to get there.

I'm on my feet, weaving through the hallways until I reach the door behind the tapestry across from my royal quarters. I listen at the door for anyone in the hallway, but it's devoid of human life. All the guards must be down at the ballroom. I slip out of the secret passage and stay in the shadows, staying close to the cold stone walls as I make my way to my father's room. I reach for the door and find it unlocked.

My heart thuds, trepidation crawling up my skin. Maybe I should go back.

Because this is *too* easy.

No guards.

Unlocked door.

Nothing in my way.

My stomach cramps, probably nerves.

I suck in a slow breath. I can do this; it's just reconnaissance.

My hand twists the door handle, and I push it open.

Silence greets me. There's a heaviness in the air in here. I close the door and slowly scan the room. It's perfectly clean, the bed made, nothing out of the ordinary.

Except for the large mirror against the wall.

It's bigger than I remember, with gold filigree around the edges. It stands on its own, clawed golden feet on each side of the bottom, keeping it erect and stately.

A chill races up my spine, goosebumps erupting along my arms the longer I look at it.

It's evil, even if I can't see the darkness emanating from it like Rowena can.

Dread pools in my stomach, mixing with the nausea as I walk closer to the mirror.

My reflection greets me in the glass. At some point, my hood fell off my head, and the dirt smeared on my face is clear to see. As I study my eyes, the picture before me changes. My hair becomes perfectly styled, my worn leather hunter's uniform transforms into kingly robes, and a thick golden crown perches upon my head.

This will be yours, but you'll have need of me to keep it.

The voice is oily and dark, and I feel as if I'm about to lose what little I ate this morning as the blackness touches my mind, repeating itself over and over again.

I take a step back, holding onto the banister of my father's bed as I force myself to focus.

No.

I don't *need* whatever this evil magic is.

I have Rowena.

I have my people.

This is *not* needed.

I cling to the fiery outrage in my chest, letting it burn away the darkness slithering inside me. It's as if it's fighting to control my mind and heart, an unseen battle I'm determined to win.

But then my stomach heaves, and I'm on my knees on the stone floor.

I cover my mouth, trying to hold in the apple turnover from Cook.

Wait . . .

My father's door swings open. My eyes travel from the polished black boots, up over the embroidered pants and tunic, and land on my father's face.

"Hello, son."

Chapter Thirty-One

An Announcement Most Dreaded

Rowena

The longer I dance, the more I know something is wrong. King Ferdinand left the room several songs ago.

Did someone get caught? Why is the king not in this room?

I've danced with several noblemen, though I doubt I'll remember more than a vague recollection of their names. I expected to dance with King Ferdinand and then slip out of the room to go destroy the mirror.

I stumble when the main doors to the ballroom slam open. The musicians falter, and conversations die as the king stalks into the room. Behind him, guards transport a golden mirror.

My heart sinks into my stomach. Bile creeps up my throat at the sight of the cursed object.

"My people," King Ferdinand shouts. "I feared my son had died after he disappeared a few days ago. Yet I was wrong. It seems as if he's been trapped in my mirror."

The guards move the mirror, setting it down next to the throne. King Ferdinand taps on the glass which ripples, revealing a man trapped inside.

Alvor.

He presses against the glass, his mouth moving, though no sound escapes.

I take a step forward, but a hand on my elbow keeps me in place. Duke Scarlett looks at me, grief in his eyes. He shakes his head, an unspoken command not to make a scene.

Gasps and whispers surround me. The heat of the ballroom is oppressive, yet my body grows colder with each passing second that I stare at Alvor's face in the mirror.

King Ferdinand's voice cuts through the murmurings. "I don't know yet who did this to my son. Who tainted their magic into something so dark and twisted that they're capable of trapping a full-grown man in a piece of glass? But I will not stand for it. I will search out the other kingdoms and find the evil person. Then we will wage war."

Heads bob, and angry voices raise in agreement with the king's bloodthirsty desires.

"My son," the king continues, "shall be forced to spend the rest of his days in this mirror, unless we can find the person who cursed him to this torturous fate. For now, I shall keep him close, and the mirror shall stay in my rooms."

The king's eyes meet mine, a dark glint unmistakable despite the distance between us. His lips twitch upward. "Any who have magic are welcome to try rescuing my son. They only need ask."

My chest seizes, airflow ceasing as I stare at the king.

He *knows.*

I tear my gaze away, meeting Duke Scarlett's grim expression. He extends his arm to me, and I cling to it. We turn, but then the king speaks, his words spreading threads of darkness through the room, some clinging to and wrapping around my chest.

"As we wait to know how to rescue Prince Alvor, I shall remarry and produce an heir to keep our kingdom stable. Which is why I have made my choice of a bride."

I stare at the polished stones on the floor. My stomach turns at the thought of a young woman marrying the king.

"Duke Scarlett, please bring that lovely woman to me. I wish to make her my wife."

No.

It wasn't meant to go this far.

We were never meant to get to this moment.

I'm frozen, my limbs iced over as fear races through my body. I don't want to get closer to the king. I don't want to move. I want to run away, back to my forest with my men and Alvor.

This has to be a nightmare.

But no. Duke Scarlett tugs on my arm, gently propelling me through the crowd that parts like the sea. My eyes move from the floor to King Ferdinand's darkened gaze, his black-tinted eyes filled with malice.

It's not until I'm at the bottom of the three steps leading up to the throne that I break out of my stupor. It's not until I meet Alvor's eyes in that mirror that I break free of the darkness wrapping around me. He's trapped behind glass, his mouth moving silently as he bangs a fist against the glass, though no sound escapes. One look at him and fire races through my bones, purging me of fear and doubt.

I will break Alvor free if it's the last thing I do.

My steps steady, my body stills its trembling, and I set my face into a neutral expression. King Ferdinand does not deserve to see *any* of my true feelings.

Duke Scarlett lets go of my arm as I ascend the steps to stand before the king. The king looks me up and down, a greedy glint in his eyes. "Hello again." His voice is quiet, carrying to me and few others, but it's laced with anger and darkness. Tendrils of it escape his mouth as he speaks. "My little huntress has come back to me? How quaint." His eyebrows lower as he glares while extending his elbow for me to loop my arm through. "Come, little huntress, let me introduce you to the court."

I arch an eyebrow. "You're not going to arrest me for not following your orders?" I flick my eyes to the mirror.

King Ferdinand smirks. "No. I have a better torture in mind for you."

I clench my jaw but resist his bait.

He steps forward, latching onto my arm, and forcefully threading it through his. My body revolts at his touch, yet I keep myself still.

He turns us toward the crowd.

"Everyone, please let me introduce you to Rowena de Frossard, niece of King Esteban De Trinanta of Rovia. We will be married in three days' time. All are invited to attend the festivities."

Gasps sound across the ballroom, but I pay them no mind. My back is straight, my face made of stone, as I stare above their heads at an elaborate chandelier.

My fingernails dig into my palms. Mother forsook her birthright when she married my father. She never claimed her royal heritage after moving to Lyriva. She was content being a lady-in-waiting and married to a common hunter, and this—this feels like throwing her decision to follow love and not money into the outhouse.

King Esteban may be my uncle, but he's never been family.

I didn't expect this move from King Ferdinand. Is it supposed to ease political worries? Because I doubt Rovia wants to claim a bandit as niece to a king.

But I should have expected something like this.

Darkness doesn't mean someone isn't intelligent—it means they're fighting on the wrong side.

I *need* to get to that mirror. Maybe I can channel my light magic into it and get Alvor out.

I shiver as King Ferdinand continues speaking, darkness spewing from his mouth like a black fog, spreading through the crowd. His words soothe the gaping mouths and surprised faces until all look serene once more. As if they've always known my parentage, that they've always respected me and treated me according to my station.

It's lies. It's deceit. It's darkness deceiving them into believing in half-truths.

The king finishes speaking, and yet I still don't have a plan. I could pull away from the king and run to the mirror, except those guards have sharp swords and I have a hooped skirt. Not great odds. My weapons and hunting leathers are in my trunk in the room I was hoping to stay in next to Duke Scarlett.

My arm is yanked as King Ferdinand turns, pulling me toward a side door. I stumble once before keeping time with him as he forces me down the hallway. We traverse through castle halls until we go up the flight of stairs that leads to the royal quarters. We reach the king's rooms, and he throws me inside.

I catch myself before I fall on the rug, straightening and turning toward him. The guards trail in behind him, putting the mirror next to the windows, Alvor's face still pressed up against the glass.

King Ferdinand stalks toward me, and I back up until my legs hit the edge of his bed. He stops a hand's breadth from me. "You will marry me or I will kill Alvor, not just leave him trapped in that mirror. Do you understand?"

I stare at him, unflinching, though the desire to look at Alvor is overwhelming. "I would rather die."

His eyes narrow. "Perfect, then you shall both die. How poetic. A tragedy that will garner more sympathy from my people. My son dying, and my new wife with the same horrible fate."

"Why?" I whisper. "Why are you letting this evil corrupt you?"

King Ferdinand shrugs, his salt-and-pepper hair and ridiculously ornate gold crown not moving an inch with the casual gesture. "What? Do you expect me to explain everything to you because you simply asked? No. My motives are my own." He turns, snapping his fingers at his guards. "Lock Lady Rowena in the queen's quarters and return the key to me. No one has access to either that room or this one without my permission."

I arch an eyebrow. "So now I'm your prisoner?"

King Ferdinand arches his eyebrows mockingly. "Did you expect anything less?"

I fold my arms. "I was looking forward to the dungeons, actually."

His lips curl. "No. I think the torture for you will be knowing I can open our connecting doors at any moment and have my way with you. It's the mental anguish that will do you in. Plus the dungeons are easy to escape. The queen's quarters . . . well, I doubt you'll want to escape without taking my mirror. Thus, you shall stay on the other side of that door." He points to an ornate door in the wall, and bile rises in my throat. I cover my mouth with my hand—the movement involuntary.

"You're despicable."

The guards walk toward me, and King Ferdinand moves to stand in front of his mirror. Alvor hammers the glass with his fists, desperation written across his face that stares at me over the king's shoulder.

He licks his lips as I walk by. "No, I'm just the evil king, darling."

Chapter Thirty-Two

A Dress Most Horrid

Three Days Until the Wedding

Rowena

I didn't sleep after King Ferdinand locked me in my room last night. So when a key turns in the lock on my door, I jump out of the bed, standing behind a chair I could use as a weapon if needed.

The door is pushed open by the king. Cook trails behind him with a tray she sets on the vanity table. The bread, cheese, and slices of fruit are tempting to my empty stomach.

Then again, I don't really trust anything from King Ferdinand, but Cook is the one delivering it, and I trust her.

Before I'm able to say anything, she's gone from the room again, leaving the king standing there, watching me with those dark eyes.

I grip the back of the chair, the wood cutting into my palms.

King Ferdinand smirks. "Eat. You'll need your strength if you're to bear me a son."

My nose wrinkles, and I throw back my shoulders. “Never.”

His eyebrow arches, and the urge to throw something at him nearly overcomes me.

“We shall see. Our seamstress will meet with you later this afternoon. Enjoy your time alone.” He saunters out of the room, and the lock on the other side of the door clicks into place.

My stomach grumbles and I retrieve the food, sitting as far away from the two doors into the room as possible.

A few hours to myself sounds nice in theory, but it’s too much time to think and run my mind in circles. I need to do something.

The bread and cheese is gone first, and as I savor the strawberries on the plate, I study the room more fully. I never found a secret passageway into here as a child, and my father never mentioned if there was one here. Maybe there isn’t.

But what better time to check?

I pull out the one dagger I had strapped to my thigh under my dress. It’s a familiar weight in my hand, a comfort to know I’m not entirely defenseless. I keep it close to my side as I slip off the bed, keeping it out of view of the doorways just in case someone barges in.

My fingers run over the walls, the mortar between stones, the holes, seams, and behind furniture. I move every tapestry, every candlestick, and every book on the small bookshelf.

Nothing.

I can’t escape. After searching every inch of this room, flipping through every book, and inspecting every inch of the walls, it’s official. I’m trapped in here.

I stare at the bookshelf, scanning the titles to see if there's something of interest for me to read. There isn't. What I really want is a book of magic, because I have no idea if my magic can help me right now. My magic isn't aggressive; it's not made for warfare, but for caring and soothing, and though it's comforting having this light inside of me, I really wish it worked in practical ways, like helping me pick a lock.

I look at the windows and can't help but sigh. They're only two hands' breadths wide. Trying to climb out of them would be an impossible feat. The stone of the palace walls is sheer, without handholds or crevices. I don't want to plummet down three stories to the ground below.

Whoever designed this castle didn't think about the potential need for escape routes from the queen's quarters, and it shows.

I grab a book and settle in the chair by the window. Might as well study the dust motes in the morning light or try to read this history book. Maybe it holds secrets untold.

Spoiler alert: It didn't have secrets. It was dry and boring, and after starting and stopping the same page fifteen times, I gave up.

So I do some . . . rearranging.

There's now a large dresser in front of the door leading to the king's room. I've made a defensive barrier around my bed with chairs and small tables, and all books have been moved off the bookshelf and are now piled at my bedside.

King Ferdinand may be waging mental warfare against me, but I'll be the one bringing the steel dagger into the fight if needed. My barricade should give me ample time to prepare for an attack.

It's only when I pick up the next history book to start reading do I hear my door unlock. The castle seamstress is let into my room. There's a white gown draped across her arms, and a young assistant trails her with hands full of thread, pins, and ribbons and undergarments.

King Ferdinand watches from the door. "Seems as if you've done some redecorating." He frowns when he sees the dresser blocking the door to his room.

I shrug. "I had some time on my hands to see if I'm any good at interior decorating. I don't think it's my strong suit, but it was an enjoyable experiment."

He glares.

I smirk.

One point for me. He's still in the running, but I'm clinging to my singular point.

The seamstress weaves through the chairs and tables until she's next to my bed. She looks over at King Ferdinand, who leans against the doorframe of the room. "We need privacy to work, Your Majesty."

The king purses his lips, eyes narrowing. "Lady Rowena, just so you are aware, we caught two poachers this morning—men I thought long dead. Imagine my surprise when they were caught hunting in my section of the forest. I'm thinking our wedding day might be a good day for their execution. What do you think?"

I lied. All the points go to King Ferdinand.

My stomach turns, my body suddenly heavy as my throat constricts.

Two of my men. It has to be.

Bile rises, and I turn away from the king before I spew acid-tinted words that would only make the situation worse. The door closes, the lock turns, enclosing me in this gilded prison cell with these women.

The tailor, Mistress Flora who has helped me make my hunting leathers, inspects me from head to toe. "We'll need to take in the waist and let out the shoulders. I forgot how muscular you are, but no matter, it's an easy fix. Maybe we'll try that new corset?"

I change into the new underthings, and as Mistress Flora babbles about the ruffles in the wedding dress, I move to pick up the corset. Mistress Flora stops talking for a moment, watching me struggle with the laces. "You have a very fine figure, Lady Rowena. That corset will do you wonders. Maybe all of that hunting has done you good."

"Rowena, please," I whisper. "Just Rowena."

I pull on the strings, trying to tighten it, but instead get my fingers tangled.

Mistress Flora clucks as she grabs a swatch of fabric from Daisy, her assistant. "You know, I about forgot who your mother was, bless her soul. I can't believe I didn't remember that you're a lady in your own right."

I shake my head, grumbling at this contraption I haven't worn in ... well, I guess I wore one yesterday. My magic flares within me, and just like when my eyes connected with Alvor that first night in the dining hall, my magic reaches out for these women.

I let it. Anything to lessen the curse on the people in the castle. I look up, staring into Mistress Flora's eyes, willing the darkness to flee from her mind. "I'm not a lady. My mother forsook her title when she married my father. She never cared about it."

Daisy whispers, "But you're the niece of King Esteban."

I shrug, then wince as I pull the strings tighter. "I've never met him, and he hasn't cared one whit about me since my mother died. I'm content being the daughter of a huntsman. It's the only role I've known."

Mistress Flora and Daisy lift the hooped skirt to maneuver it over my head, but I hold out my hand to stop them.

Something isn't right.

I can't breathe.

I tug at the knot I just made. It won't budge, and as I stare down at the white corset, I notice something I hadn't seen before.

A black mist hovers over the fabric.

"It's cursed . . ." I squeak out with the last of my breath.

Mistress Flora's eyes go wide. With astonishing speed, she pulls out a pair of scissors from her skirt and snips at the strings binding it together.

It doesn't rip.

My lungs burn.

"Daisy, get over here and help me pull this thing off of Lady Rowena."

The girl scurries over, and as I try to pull the fabric away from my body, the two women take a ragged cut edge and tug on it.

My magic flares, white light blinding me as it rushes through my body and out through my hands.

We all stumble and fall to the floor.

The two women each hold a piece of the fabric; the rest lies on the ground beneath me.

"What in the world was that?" Mistress Flora asks after a moment.

I pick up the fabric and walk over to the fire, throwing it in and watching it burn.

"That, my ladies," I say, "was a cursed object. Thank you for helping me escape it."

They blink slowly, shock written across their face.

"Well then," Mistress Flora murmurs. "We can still make you a dress fit for a queen, even without . . . that."

"I don't think I want it," I murmur.

A frown mars the seamstress's face. "Even so. The king has named you a noble, and you are to marry him. We'll have your dress flaunt your beauty to the best of my abilities. Each queen should start her own fashion trend, you know. It's what all queens do when they assume the throne."

Goosebumps race over my skin. "I don't want the throne," I rasp.

Except . . . I do.

I just wish Alvor was the one wearing the crown.

Chapter Thirty-Three

A Father Most Greedy

Alvor

Everything is gray. I've never hated a color before, but I hate this one. The only light in the space comes from whatever is on the other side of the mirror.

But I can't look out. Not when the only thing I'm going to see is my father gloating over his coins or hurting Rowena.

I slam my fists against the ground. It feels like stone, but it doesn't actually have texture to it. Just blackness.

It's as if I'm suspended in nothing, my body frozen in time, yet I can still move and think, and time passes as achingly slowly as it would on the other side of the mirror.

There's a tapping sound, but I don't turn. I know who it is.

"Alvor, would you like to count the coins with me? I'm sure you'd like to see how much I squeeze from the nobles' pockets as they stay here for the festivities."

Though no one can hear what I say, I unfortunately have no problem hearing my father's gloating ramblings.

I lean my head back, pulling forward a memory of Rowena as coins clink in the background.

"Prince Alvor, I challenge you to an archery competition." Rowena's voice is full of bravado as she stands in front of me and the other young squires. They chuckle, and I can see why. She's in a dress, a bow and arrows clenched in her hand, her hair braided away from her face. She's so . . . young.

"Rowena, I don't have time for an archery competition right now," I hiss.

Her nose scrunches. "Afraid you'll lose?"

Oh, I know I'll lose. Rowena spends hours of her time in the archery range with her father. If it was swords, now that's another matter. "I just. . . I'm busy."

She looks around at the empty courtyard. "With what? I know you're done with your training for the morning. What's the harm in a little competition?"

I glance at the two boys beside me then back at Rowena, hoping she'll pick up on my hint. But she's oblivious. Thirteen-year-olds don't pick up on context clues very well.

A sigh escapes me. "Fine. One match."

The boys around me start heckling as we walk toward the archery range behind the castle. They haven't seen what Rowena can do, so I just hope I can keep my dignity intact.

Maybe I can actually hit the target this time.

Rowena sets up a target twenty paces away. Good, I should be able to hit that.

"Royalty first?" Rowena says as she hands me the bow and an arrow.

I frown. Why does she insist on not calling herself a royal? She's the niece of a king. She's just as royal as I am.

"Fine."

I aim, pull back, and . . . it lands in the grass.

Jeers erupt from our small audience. I hold back biting words as I hand the bow to Rowena.

She narrows her eyes. "Did you miss on purpose?"

My cheeks heat. "No."

Her eyebrows arch, but then she lines herself up and . . . hits a perfect bullseye.

Instead of cheers like I expect from my fellow squires, all I hear is silence.

Then I hear words that send a fiery rage through me. "I bet it was luck. No girl should be able to shoot like that. No man will want a girl who can outshoot him."

I spin on my heels, fist flying into the face of the young man with a name I will purposefully forget from this day on. "And no woman will want a man who can't appreciate her strengths."

"Alvor, are you listening to me?" My father's voice breaks through my memory, turning my smile into a frown.

I turn around, fold my arms and glare.

"Oh good, so I do have your attention. Just wanted you to know that I've now captured four of that girl's supporters. I'm hoping to raid the forest to find the rest of them."

I roll my eyes, but dread pools in my stomach.

"I'm still not sure whether I want you to hang after the wedding too. We shall see. It'll be a day worth remembering, though, seeing as I'll be marrying Robin Hood, and her band of merry men will die as she watches. Ah yes, what a day to look forward to."

I turn around again. I can't stand him.

I'd rather face this darkness than his face.

Chapter Thirty-Four

A Comb Most Cursed

Two Days Until the Wedding

Rowena

I watch the dust motes in the beam of sunlight flicker.

Being this tired is not good for my mental state and trying to plan my escape.

I squeeze my dagger tighter, sinking into my chair behind my barrier.

The lock clicks, a sound I dread and love at the same time. Cook slips through the door, a tray of food just like yesterday's in hand. I barely spare her a glance, my gaze fixed upon the king who lurks in the doorway. He's dressed in his finery, his crown atop his head and a smirk on his lips.

Once upon a time, I thought that smirk reminded me of Alvor. No longer. The evil has twisted King Ferdinand until he's barely recognizable. The dark misty magic doesn't cling to him like it does the others—it's in his eyes. They're dark, soul-sucking, and make my skin crawl as he watches me.

Cook curtsies and leaves, taking my empty tray from yesterday with her.

I'm still, ready to strike if King Ferdinand comes closer, my dagger hidden in my skirt.

He holds out his hand, and a guard places a small box in it. He walks forward toward the vanity. I've never been more grateful for my barricade than in this moment.

There will be grooves left in my palms from my dagger's hilt after this, but I'm ready, coiled to spring at a moment's notice.

"A gift for my future bride. Though I think our wedding day will have the most presents. Have you heard that I've found all the rebels led by Robin Hood? Of course not, you haven't left this room. Well, I've found them. Their punishments shall be enacted after the ceremony."

He places the box on my vanity, then turns, flicking his cloak behind him as he walks out the door without looking back.

A guard closes it.

Click.

I let my magic loose inside me, mapping out where the people are behind my door. Their white souls are tinged black, coated with the curse from the king.

Except for him.

All King Ferdinand's soul looks like is a lump of coal, dark and smoking.

I wait until they retreat down the hallway before weaving through my barricade to get to the vanity.

I don't touch the gift and instead eat half of the breakfast. There was no dinner yesterday, and I don't expect any today.

My stomach grumbles after a few bites of bread and cheese. I only eat two strawberries before setting the tray aside. Might as well satisfy my curiosity now. It's not like I have anything else to do today.

I tug at the red satin ribbon around the white box, slowly unraveling it.

I tug the lid off to find a . . . comb?

My magic flares within my chest, rushing to my hand, and blasting light at the object. It flies through the air, hits the stone wall, and clatters to the floor.

I stare at my fingers. What in the world is happening with my magic?

I creep over to the comb, and as I get closer, it begins to disintegrate. Black mist lifts off its teeth as they dissolve into dust. My magic pulses, and I pull away from the darkness floating through the air. It hits the ceiling and soaks into the stones, leaving a dark spot at odds with the rest of the gray stonework.

Apparently, my magic doesn't like cursed objects. Which bodes well for breaking the curse on the mirror.

But at what cost? And can my magic do more than explode cursed things?

Because I'd really like to get Alvor out of that mirror before it explodes.

Chapter Thirty-Five

A Day Most Depressing

One Day Until the Wedding

Rowena

I'm going to go insane. Positively bonkers. I haven't left this room in almost three days, and I'm going to marry an insane, evil king tomorrow.

I mean, when did my life get so crazy? Wasn't it enough that I was a woman huntress hiding away the king's enemies in the woods and acting as a bandit?

Yeah. That should have been enough crazy for one lifetime.

I'd use my dagger to whittle something with a chair leg or banister from the bed, but I actually kind of like the decorations in here, and I'd hate to destroy them only to have to restore them when Alvor is on the throne again.

Alvor.

I miss him.

I let a tear fall down my cheek as I stare at the ceiling.

It's hopeless. I don't know what I'm doing. I have absolutely no clue how to save him or our people, and if I try to leave, others will get hurt.

I hate when people get hurt.

The weight on my chest gets heavier as more tears stream down my face. My limbs are useless, my body numb, my mind overwhelmed with the bleakest prospects of the future.

I tilt my head to the side, looking at the book lying open on the mattress beside me. It's a history book, the contents the dry-as-dirt kind. But this one had a secret hidden in its depths.

When Solwain gifted humans magic, he warned of opposition. He taught that there is always a darkness to oppose light. Where great light thrives shall also be found great darkness. Many have speculated about the meaning of his warning, yet no clear guidance has been discerned from his words.

There is so much darkness in King Ferdinand. Does that mean he has great potential for light?

Is he really just cursed to be evil?

Is Alvor the light meant to defeat his father's evil?

There are so many questions, and so few answers.

Despair creeps into my heart as the hours tick by, ever moving closer to the moment I'm supposed to marry the king.

There's a tapping on the door, and then the lock turns.

I sit up, dagger hidden in my lap under my skirts.

Cook walks in, a small plate in her hands. It looks like an apple turnover, but what I'm struck by is the look on her face. Her face is white, not rosy-cheeked like normal. Her eyes are wide, her lips thin. When her gaze lands on mine, her eyebrows rise a fraction of an inch, her eyes going even wider.

My shoulders stiffen.

Then King Ferdinand speaks. "I thought I'd be generous to my future bride. I'm guessing it is your magic that allows you to resist the mirror's curse. So I felt merciful today and decided to offer you the chance to escape fighting me and the darkness every day. If you eat the apple turnover, which I know is Alvor's favorite, you may enter eternal slumber, something your men and my son will experience soon. Or you may not eat it and live another day, allowing you the chance to marry and submit to me." His eyes narrow. "The choice is yours."

My skin crawls, revulsion running through me as Cook and the king leave, locking the door behind me.

A dark mist rises from the turnover sitting on my vanity. The warmth of my magic jolts through me. I raise my arm to study my fingers when light shoots across the room. It shapes itself into an arrow, spearing into the turnover and obliterating it.

Turns out I don't have a choice anymore, not that I would have taken *that* one.

But . . . my light turned into an arrow.

It shot the darkness.

Light and dark, two opposites. Both powerful in their own right.

One protective, one destructive.

A vague idea forms itself in my mind, and as I lie back down on my bed, I let it simmer.

Chapter Thirty-Six

A Memory Most Treasured

Alvor

I can't seem to sleep in the mirror. My mind won't quiet, so instead I relive my memories with Rowena. They play out in my mind, keeping the darkness at bay, as I recall all the reasons I love her.

The first time I remember playing with Rowena I was around the age of five. We went to the kennels and sat with the puppies while her father watched us. She was three and giggled as the dogs licked her face.

When I was eight, our mothers decided we needed to learn to dance. They appointed us partners. It was the worst torture for an eight-year-old boy.

What I wouldn't give to dance with Rowena now.

When I was ten, my father allowed me to train with Rowena under her father, learning how to hunt with a hawk. Rowena's hawk outperformed mine every single time. I didn't know she had magic, and I hated her for how she was constantly better than me at everything.

The fateful night when I was twelve, our mothers were on their way back from a social event, and there was an accident with their carriage. I don't remember the details. I just remember finding Rowena crying in our favorite hiding spot at the edge of the forest, nestled against the tree trunk.

I sat next to her, and we wept together. She reached out and grabbed my hand, and it was everything I needed in that moment.

Rowena has always been there, and for once I'd like to show up for her.

But as my father wakes up, noises sounding from his room, I know one thing for certain:

Today is his wedding day, and I will do everything in my power to make sure it doesn't happen.

Chapter Thirty-Seven

A Wedding Most Detestable

Day of the Wedding

Rowena

The silky fabric slides over my skin, reminding me of a snake stalking its prey. It feels as restrictive as if I were caught in the trap of said reptile.

The dress is gorgeous, but everything about today makes me sick. I could barely stomach the bread and jam Cook brought me this morning. I ate a few bites, and I'm now regretting it.

"You look beautiful, Lady Rowena," Mistress Flora comments as she straightens the train of my dress.

All I can muster is a small smile. As I look in the mirror, I grimace. My face says I am anything but happy.

Mistress Flora steps back. "All finished. We're to escort you to the guards. The king would like me to remind you to not run away from your guards or else the execution will take place before the wedding."

My stomach clenches.

I *can't* lose anyone else.

Somehow, I will escape from this monster.

Mistress Flora and Daisy walk out of the room at my sides, escorting me to the lowest level of the castle where guards assume their places. I grip my skirts and exit the castle. When a guard offers their hand to assist me into the carriage, I refuse.

A fire burns in my chest as we ride through the streets. The chapel's tall steeple draws closer, along with the scaffolding beside it made for the gallows. My heart beats in time with the horses hooves, thundering inside of me, as I'm drawn closer to my doom.

I hate being a damsel in distress. If only I had my dagger or a bow. But I couldn't figure out how to hide my dagger while getting dressed in front of Mistress Flora. So here I am, weaponless, with unpredictable magic and a small inkling of an idea of how to escape.

We pull into the courtyard outside the chapel. Nobles sit in chairs opposite the gallows where six men stand, ropes secured around their necks.

I bite my lip to keep from crying out. My men are standing there, waiting to die while I'm stuck in this ridiculously fluffy wedding dress with hair piled atop of my head and an aching neck.

The sorrow is replaced by a fire in my bones, my magic coursing through me. I don't know how, but I hold it back, letting it strengthen each of my steps as I move forward through the crowd to where King Ferdinand stands with the priest.

Behind the king is the cursed mirror, Alvor's face pressed against the glass, his eyes watching me.

Despite the absolute despair coursing through me in this moment, I don't see an ounce of that on Alvor's face. He looks almost… smug.

My feet keep moving, and I keep my eyes on Alvor. I can't look at my men without crying, and with his face in front of me, I think I might be brave enough to do anything.

When King Ferdinand holds out his hand for me to grasp, I ignore it, instead clasping my hands together and holding them at my waist.

When I marry Alvor, I'm going to have flowers in my hand. That's right. I *am* going to marry him. I just have to get to him first.

"Lady Rowena?" King Ferdinand asks, his eyebrow arched as he holds out his hand to me.

I look down at it. It's wrinkly, calloused, and being this close means I can see the black tint to the veins under his skin.

No.

I will not touch him.

I would rather die.

My eyes flick up. Three steps.

I hike up my skirts and kick my leg, hitting King Ferdinand's knee. He curses as he crumples to the ground while reaching for me, but he's too slow. I've already reached the mirror.

My magic thrums and pounces when my fingers graze the cold metal of the gilded frame.

There's a yell from behind me, but it's too late.

I slam my palm on the glass, channeling my rage, indignation, and most importantly my love for Alvor and this kingdom into my hand, begging the light to flow from me so I can free my prince.

The light responds, flaring around me—and I'm sucked into the mirror.

Chapter Thirty-Eight

A Duel Most Daring

Alvor

I fall to the ground, but there's no time to waste. I leap upward, but Rowena is nowhere to be seen.

I spin around.

She's gone.

Wait, no. She's in the mirror.

There's a cry of despair, and it takes a moment to realize it's coming from me.

A chuckle sounds behind me, and I turn to see my father standing in his richest clothes. "Well, it seems you can get someone out of the mirror as long as there is someone to trade places with them."

All I see is red as my fist collides with his nose.

My father stumbles, catching himself on the next step as he holds his nose, blood dripping down his hand. "Guards, arrest Alvor for assaulting the king."

No one moves, and I meet the eyes of every man in the area, each of whom I know by name.

I might have been cursed, but I still kept up with my daily guard training.

I turn to the captain of the king's guard standing to the side of the proceedings. "Leroy, hand me a sword, immediately."

He bows his head and relinquishes his own weapon. The handle slides into my grip with ease, a familiar friend.

I fall into a defensive stance. "Shall we duel for the crown, Father?"

He scoffs, wiping blood on his sleeve and ruining the fabric in the process. "I am the king. I duel no one." Then he turns to Leroy. "I hereby banish you for treason."

Leroy arches his eyebrows under his helm, but he doesn't show any other flicker of emotion.

Duke Wessex steps forward through the crowd, Duke Scarlett at his side. "I support Prince Alvor's challenge for the throne."

Warmth blossoms in my chest. William chose a wonderful future father-in-law.

My uncle speaks up, echoing the duke's words.

Then another, and another.

I can't see magic like Rowena can, but it's almost as if before my eyes each nobleman returns to themselves, their shoulders straightening, and outrage becoming apparent on their faces.

My father quakes as he studies the agitated crowd. "What is the meaning of this?" he shouts.

I whistle, and the noise cuts through the chatter. "Release those men from the gallows. No one shall die today."

"No one?" My father snarls as he pulls his sword from his belt. "How about you?"

I shake my head. "No. You sent the woman I love to kill me, Father. I will not die before I'm reunited with her once more."

"She's pathetic." He spits into the dirt. "She couldn't kill a man even if she tried."

My eyes narrow. "No. Rowena de Frossard has more integrity and nobility than anyone in this kingdom can claim. Her power comes not from fear, but from the light within her."

We lunge for each other, the metal of our swords ringing as we collide. It's always been an even match between us. But today, I'm filled with light.

Chapter Thirty-Nine

A Mirror Most Dark

Rowena

I'm in a gray wasteland. Dark mist swirls around me. The fire of my magic heats me from within, stoking itself into a raging fire as I take in my surroundings.

In the blink of an eye, the fire within me spreads. My wedding dress is bathed in light until it takes on the shape of my hunting leathers. A bow made of light is in one hand; an arrow that glows the brightest white appears in the other.

Wow. Didn't realize my magic could do that.

On instinct, I shove my magic out through my feet, trying to see if there's anything around me like I do when I'm in the forest. Instead, I hear a sharp, keening noise, like the scratch of nails on a chalkboard or the wail of a woman.

My surroundings move, humanoid shapes of darkness emerging from the fog. The urge to shoot one grows.

So I do.

It hits the shadow, which dissolves with a relieved sigh.

Weird, but okay.

I keep shooting. The nice thing about my magic bow is that it reloads itself with magic arrows. I don't have to reach back for my quiver or anything.

My confidence grows with each shadow destroyed, until the landscape is empty. My arm aches, but I keep shooting.

I'm a huntress once more.

When nothing moves and the landscape has brightened, I turn back to the mirror's face.

I can't see beyond it.

I stare at the light reflecting from my bow and arrow.

Then the mirror quakes. Darkness spirals from it, reaching for me with inky tendrils, a deep redness behind them reminding me of the color of blood.

No.

I shoot with a speed that makes me want to weep. The strain on my muscles and the strength leaking from me with every white arrow that leaves my bow has me quivering, until finally the mirror stills.

I pull back, trembling, as I aim one last bolt straight at the glass.

My fingers let go as I exhale. The arrow flies true, hitting the center of the glass. It cracks, and the keening from earlier returns.

I rush forward and touch the glass. It slices my finger.

It's only then that I remember what Doctor Standford said about blood.

I wait, letting a single drop pool on my fingertip. I channel my magic into it until the red drop glows. I touch it to the glass. It soaks into the smooth surface and then spreads, one drop covering every inch of glass. I push on it again, and the mirror shatters, my hand breaking through. I catch a glimpse of sunshine as I stumble through the opening.

Exhaustion tugs at me, and as arms catch me before hitting the ground, I fall into a deep sleep.

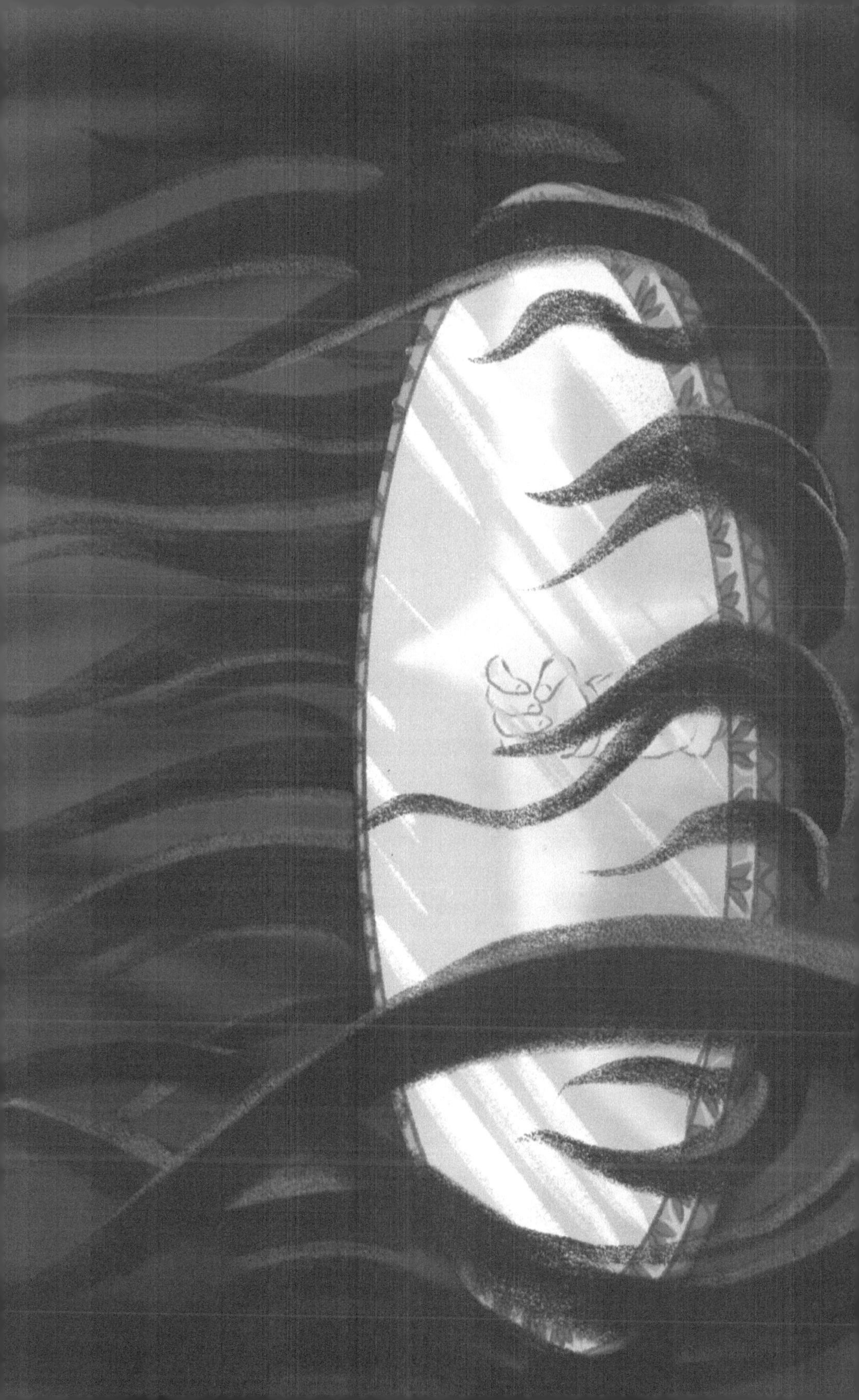

Chapter Forty

A Day Most Saved

Alvor

Gasps sound from the crowd, distracting me from my duel with my father. In the moment of weakness, he lunges for my left side, and I can barely parry the blow.

"Finish it!" The shout comes from a familiar voice, and Little John's encouragement gives me the extra dose of energy I need. I push my father back, striking like a snake and popping his sword from his grip. I hold the tip of my blade against his neck. "Yield."

Father's eyes flick behind me, his shoulders sagging as if all energy has been drained from him. Then, he lunges for me, his hands outstretched as if to grab me.

My blade moves, slicing across his cheek as I jump backward and out of his reach.

His hand moves to his face as he cries out, a sound that wrenches my heart.

"It's over, Father," I grit out as I move my quaking blade down from his neck to his heart.

He blinks slowly before pulling his hand away and inspecting the blood coating his fingertips. "Fine. But don't expect answers from me, son. You have sealed your doom this day." He lifts his hands, his arms quaking. "I yield."

Little John and Stue appear at my side, ropes in hand.

"Tie him up," I say. "He is under arrest for treason and use of dark magic."

The crowd gasps again.

Father growls. "You can't prove it." But there's fear in his eyes, and he keeps glancing behind me.

"I absolutely can, and I will in the court of law. For now, Little John, please escort my father to the dungeons."

Little John nods. "Turn around, Prince Alvor."

I quirk my eyebrows, my heart still pounding, my mind racing through everything that needs to be done, starting with finding a way to save Rowena.

Except when I turn around, there she is.

Leroy cradles her in his arms as he sits on the ground, surrounded by shards of glass.

Dale and Much flank him, with Marius behind them.

Gingerly, I step over to the glass pieces. "What happened?" I whisper as I push a strand of hair out of Rowena's face. It's a mystery to me, but somehow she's changed from her wedding dress into her hunting leathers.

"The mirror cracked, sir," Leroy explains. "As I turned to inspect it a hand reached out, and Lady Rowena fell through it. I caught her as the mirror pieces rained down on us."

"Thank you for catching her."

He nods. "Your Highness, when Lady Rowena entered the mirror, a moment later it was as if a darkness over my mind was removed and I could think again. I was so shocked I couldn't do anything for a moment. When I finally processed what was happening, I realized I didn't want to follow through on the king's orders."

I stand, though all I want to do is scoop Rowena up. But this needs to be solved now. I step toward the crowd. "Do you all feel as if you can think clearly again?"

There's a chorus of agreements.

She did it.

I crouch next to Leroy and scoop Rowena up in my arms, kissing her brow when it wrinkles for a moment. I turn back to the crowd. "I invite everyone to return to their homes. There shall be no wedding or festivities today. When Lady Rowena has recovered, we shall gather for my coronation and an explanation of events. Until then, know that you owe your lives to this woman in my arms. Without her, I would not be here, and the darkness would still plague us all."

Marius steps forward. "How can I help, Your Highness?"

I walk down the steps, slowly and steady. "Find us a carriage?"

He nods and races ahead of me. Dale and Much walk over to my side.

"Much, can you find Doctor Standford? I imagine Rowena could use some magical support."

Much nods, walking into the crowd. Dale steps up. "I'll head to the castle. She'll need food to help her recovery."

I nod. "Thank you. I hadn't thought of that."

Dale strides away, and as the crowd parts for me and the sleeping woman in my arms, I can't help but send up prayers of gratitude to the heavens.

A carriage pulls up in front of me, Marius in the driver's seat.

I slip inside, holding Rowena on my lap and cradling her head against my chest. She's limp, and though her hair still smells of lilacs, I'm afraid that it took everything from her to destroy the mirror.

Joy wars against the fear in my chest.

I bury my nose in Rowena's hair, pulling her more tightly against me as my adrenaline begins to fade.

My body trembles, and I place a shaky kiss on her forehead. "I love you, Rowena. Please come back to me."

Her breathing is shallow, and her eyelashes flutter but don't open.

My body quakes, and I let the trembling overtake me, the trauma of the past few days running its course through me. I cling to Rowena as we travel over every bump in the road and until we pull into the courtyard.

"I love you," I murmur into her hair as I shift, getting ready to disembark from the carriage.

Rowena sighs, a noise that brings peace to my heart. Whatever happens, we'll make it through this; we'll take on each day together.

Chapter Forty-One

A Dream Most Real

Rowena

Warm fingers stroke my cheek, and I inhale the spiced scent of a certain prince.

I force my eyes open, and the room comes into focus. I take inventory of my body, which seems to be lying on a comfortable sofa, my head resting in a handsome prince's lap.

Definitely feels like a dream. Maybe I should close my eyes again and revel in it before I need to wake up.

"Are you awake, love?"

I peek through my eyelashes before opening my eyes more fully, slowly taking in every inch of Alvor's face. He's clean shaven again, his smooth skin highlighting his high cheekbones. His hair is combed back, the adorable swoop in the front of his hair looking like it needs a good tousling. His lips—yep, they're still utterly kissable, and I focus on them for an extra second before moving to his blue eyes, which are crinkled with mirth.

Then my mind catches up with me, and I gasp. "Did I do it? Did we win?"

Alvor grins, his thumb stroking my cheek as his hand cradles my head. "Yes. You broke the mirror and its enchantment, though I'm sad a kiss from my true love wasn't the ultimate solution."

I sigh and move my hand from my lap up to his chest, playing with the ties on the front of his tunic. "That would have been amazing, and a much easier solution, but nothing has ever been easy with you, princeling."

He chuckles, and I enjoy feeling the rumble of it in his chest. "Are we back to name calling?"

I tug on the ties of his shirt. "Maybe?"

"Then can I call you my betrothed?"

My hand stills and I sit up, only briefly taking note of the maid in the far corner of the sitting room we're in before focusing on the man in front of me. "Alvor?"

He tilts his head, his eyes soft as he looks at me. "Yes, my love?"

"Is this your way of proposing? I'm barely awake after whatever that was." I wave my hand in the air, hissing at him. "I don't even know what day or time it is, Alvor!"

He chuckles and grabs my flailing hand and kisses my palm, then the inside of my wrist.

Suddenly, all of my concerns are nonexistent.

"Rowena, it was torture being in that mirror. When I was stuck, I tuned out my father's vile filth by remembering every moment of my life that I shared with you. You were the light that got me through the darkest days of my existence. I promised myself I wouldn't waste a moment with you if we made it through everything. So, Rowena de Frossard, will you marry me and be my wife forever? Will you help me bring light and prosperity back to our kingdom? With you by my side I know I can do anything, and I can be the good man I want to become."

Tears stream down my cheeks, and he wipes them away as he cradles my face. "I love you, Rowena. Please, marry me?"

I nod and reach for his face, my fingers caressing his cheeks and the crinkles created by the wide smile on his face before weaving into his hair. I tug him closer, my nose brushing against his as I whisper my answer. "Yes, Alvor. I'll marry you, bring magic back to our kingdom, and love you forever."

My heart races, and my stomach swoops as Alvor kisses me with every ounce of wonder and joy I feel for having fallen for my no-longer-cursed prince.

Chapter Forty-Two

An Epilogue Most Swoony

Alvor

My knuckles tap against the wooden desk. My eyes burn from staring at these ledgers for so long. They make absolutely no sense. It's been a month since my father's arrest, and I've lowered taxes to as low as I can possibly go to cover basic expenses. I've returned stolen property, reinstated fair tariffs, given to every orphanage and family in the entire kingdom. Yet there is still a large unexplained sum of money sitting in the vaults.

All I've found is one singular entry, with no name. Just ten thousand gold coins deposited into our vault with no way of knowing where they've come from.

Father has been tight-lipped. He's a shell of a man. After the mirror broke, he retreated into himself. I still can't tell whether he was cursed or acting of his own greed, and I don't care to spend hours trying to get answers.

It feels as if I've lost my father for good, joining Rowena in being an orphan.

Except, I can't really say that, because I've had so many people step up since that fateful day a month ago. My uncle, Duke Scarlett, has taken on a fatherly role in my life as my chief advisor. The merry men have been welcomed onto my advisory council and have also become the brothers I never had but always wanted.

Then there's Rowena. My Robin Hood gave up her vigilante duties immediately and assumed the role of an influential lady in my courts with surprising ease. She wears fine dresses she designed with Mistress Flora that are sleek and modern, yet allow her to shoot a bow and arrow with ease. Though, I still catch her gallivanting around with her merry men in her hunting leathers. They like to go to the villages and give them my gold coins. I think they feel like they're still robbing the rich to feed the poor even though I'm literally giving them the coins to give away.

But who am I to spoil their fun?

I'm just the guy who has to deal with all the paperwork of running a kingdom.

So. Much. Paperwork.

A knock on the door sends a shock of relief through me. Please let it be a distraction from this mind-bending mess. I clear my throat. "Come in."

The door swings open, and the woman of my dreams walks in. She stops in front of my desk, her hands on her hips, a frown marring her beautiful brow. "Alvor, I'm tired of waiting. Let's get married."

I chuckle and lean back in my leather chair. "My love, we're getting married tomorrow."

Rowena huffs and plops into the chair across from my desk, her arms folded petulantly as she slouches and glowers at me. "Tomorrow is too far away."

I arch an eyebrow. "Were you spending time with William and Marian again?"

She waves her hand in the air. "They're so sickeningly in love. Ridiculous newlyweds. They can't stop kissing, and it makes me want to run away and kiss your face off and not worry about the consequences."

I tent my fingers and tamp down the laughter that wants to sneak out. "I'm not the one who instituted a kissing ban."

Rowena points at me. "It's your ridiculously handsome face. I can't keep my head around you. And you're the one who insisted we needed to send official invites to the surrounding kingdoms, while I just wanted to elope." She refolds her arms, huffing and staring at my bookshelves.

I shrug. "With all of the upheaval, I don't think anyone would have taken well to us getting married the day after we deposed my father."

She blows out a breath, pushing a stray curl out of her eyes. "Yes, yes, yes, I know logically it makes sense. But I just want to get married already."

I rub my fingers over my lips to disguise my smile. "I promise, I feel the same."

Her eyes light up. "So you'll elope with me?"

I laugh. I can't help it. She's been so patient with me. Though she insisted we institute a kissing ban after we got caught by her merry men for the tenth time, and they wouldn't stop teasing her. I've never gone a day without knowing Rowena loves me. Her love has been the steady rock I've needed as we've put our kingdom back together.

"Tomorrow we can elope."

She glares. "It's not eloping if we go to the wedding *we* planned."

I shrug. "I can call it whatever I want, because it doesn't really matter. Tomorrow you're going to be mine forever."

Some of the tension in her shoulders loosens. "Fine. I guess I can wait until tomorrow if you keep saying sweet things."

I grin. "Perfect. Now, want to help me solve another mystery?"

She nods. "Is this about the large sum you can't trace?"

I nod. "I can't figure it out. I've gone through all of the records from the last five years. I have no idea where this came from."

Her eyebrows raise. "Wait? Five years ago? That's when your father got the mirror. Do you think they're tied together?"

I lean back, mulling over the timeline and implications. "You know, my love, I think you might be right."

Her eyes go wide. "Alvor, do you think they paid your father to spread the darkness?"

I blow out a sharp breath. "Wouldn't surprise me. His greed had overtaken him by then, and he was still grieving."

"I don't think we'll find the culprit, then. I'm not sure where it came from, and I think they'll continue to hide their tracks." She stands, walks around the desk, and reaches for my hands. I grip hers, obeying her gentle tug urging me to stand. She wraps her arms around my waist, and I weave my fingers into her silky hair as I cradle her in this sweet embrace.

"Alvor, I think it's time to let it go. You've done all you can to fix your father's mess. Now, we move forward, our kingdom stronger for your light and goodness. Whoever wanted to destroy us failed, and we'll be stronger for it. *You* are stronger for it."

This kissing ban is the worst, because all I want to do right now is tell her with my lips just how much her light and goodness mean to me. But I resist. Guess I'll need to use actual words instead. "You're amazing, Rowena. You always know exactly what I need to hear."

Her contented sigh soothes my worries, and I hold her for several moments before her fingers start to move. They find the part of my side that is ticklish, and she unleashes havoc.

I break away, taking a step back, but not before she reaches up and bops my nose. "That's right, I do. Now stop looking so handsome, princeling. You're far too tempting."

I tug on one of her curls, wrapping the end around my finger. "You're one to talk. And what are you going to call me once I'm crowned king tomorrow?"

Rowena flounces to the door of my study before turning back, her hair falling like a riotous waterfall to her waist, a smirk growing on her lips. "Husband."

Wondering how long the kissing ban lasts for? Find out in the exclusive bonus chapter available to my newsletter subscribers. Subscribe through the QR code below.

Subscribe to M.K. Felix's Newsletter

Want to read William and Marian's story? Newsletter subscribers get the eBook of *Lady Scarlett: A Retelling of the Highwayman* for free. Keep reading for a sneak peek of their story.

LADY SCARLETT

PROLOGUE

Lady Marian Wessex

My pale-pink dress is at odds with my dour mood. Though there isn't anything I can do about the color, seeing as King Ferdinand forbade us from wearing mourning blacks for Prince Alvor, I don't have to smile.

The desire to smile is nonexistent today. Nothing about this gathering at the king's castle encourages me to feel anything but contempt and sadness.

The young men around me are sniveling, the women are simpering, and it all feels like too much. I haven't even heard the king speak yet, but I know it'll just make today worse. I always leave the castle morose, and spending time here makes it hard to think. I'm blaming it on the overly perfumed women and the choking colognes the men wear.

The doors of the ballroom are thrown open, and in waltzes King Ferdinand, a monstrous golden crown atop his head and red robes with golden trim and lace covering every inch of the fabric.

It's gaudy, and I hate it.

The room falls silent, and the buzzing in my mind quiets, only to be replaced by a thick fog as King Ferdinand speaks.

"My friends. I appreciate all who have expressed their condolences at the loss of my son. It is truly . . . tragic."

It really is tragic. Prince Alvor was the only kind man in the courts.

My nose starts to tingle as my eyes sting.

"Seeing as I no longer have an heir, it is time for me to remarry. Our kingdom has been without a queen for too long. Which is why I will be choosing a bride from among the nobility of our people."

The rest of King Ferdinand's words flow past my ears without me hearing them.

A bride from among the nobility.

That could be me.

My stomach churns, and I lift my hand to cover my mouth.

Quiet clapping sounds around me, and though I don't know what we're clapping for, I reluctantly join in.

"As we are to soon have a series of balls as I find my future wife, I will dismiss you all. Do not forget to settle your accounts with my steward as you leave today."

Heads bob as the sea of nobility exits the ballroom, not a complaint that we came here for a simple announcement among them.

Father grips my arm tightly. "We must hurry, Marian."

"Why?" I ask.

He shakes his head, frantically looking around him. "I will speak of it later. For now, let us leave."

My brows furrow, but I keep my complaints and questions to myself.

We're ushered out of the castle after Father pays his gold coin for attending the function. It's a recent change that King Ferdinand instated, citing it necessary to pay for the lavish parties he throws for his nobles. The party we didn't even get to participate in tonight.

Father ushers me into the carriage, and when the door closes, he lets out a heavy breath. He wipes his forehead with his handkerchief and watches the window with apprehension.

"What's wrong?" I ask.

Father takes a deep breath. "I've arranged for you to marry Prince Caladen of Rovia."

My jaw drops. "You have done *what*?"

Father keeps his gaze trained on the window. "It's a good thing, too. I do not wish you to be among the potential brides for King Ferdinand. When we get home, you shall pack up your things and I shall gather your dowry items. We'll head for the border tomorrow. We should arrive in Rovia the following day."

"But I don't even know him—"

Father's eyes turn on me. "No, but you shall do as you're told. It's for the best."

I bite my tongue. How many times have we attended court functions because it's "for the best"? I don't entirely trust that sentiment, especially when it takes a decision out of my hands.

If only I could escape all of this and choose a husband for myself.

I stare out the window of our carriage, unwilling to talk to Father, let alone look at him.

The trees are more entertaining, what with their majestic height. A flash of brown moves through the leaves, but I lose sight of it as we continue on the worn dirt road.

Father should be able to afford more comfortable carriages. We're to travel all the way to Rovia, and unfortunately my desire to not feel every hole or bump in the road will be unmet. My fingers clench in my lap. Marrying Prince Caladen of Rovia has never been a part of my plan for my life. Also, something must be wrong with him if he's willing to marry the daughter of a duke in a neighboring kingdom. He has princesses from other kingdoms to choose from, yet he's willing to settle for me?

Nope. Something must be wrong with him. Could I make a marriage to a stranger work? Yes. But I'd rather not.

My fingers play with the lace trim on my dress. I brush off a spot of dust on my lap. If only it was that easy to brush away the feelings of grief and confusion plaguing my mind.

Prince Alvor is dead, and though I wasn't in love with him, he was never unkind to me. I had hoped we could have even become friends one day. Now there is no chance of finding a kind suitor in Lyriva; maybe that's why Father has us traveling to Rovia. With Prince Alvor's death . . . there's no one left for me that qualifies as good enough in Father's eyes.

Father's feet tap impatiently against the floor of the carriage. "Marian . . ." he whines.

My nose presses against the glass as I shift as far away from Father as possible. The carriage jolts, and I stumble forward as we come to a halt.

"What is going on out there?" Father mutters.

I bite my tongue, holding in the sassy retort that would point out the obvious.

The unfamiliar voices from outside draw me to the carriage door, and my fingers brush the handle.

"Don't you dare open that door, Marian," Father scolds. "I will take care of this."

My eyes roll to the ceiling of the carriage. Yet, I'm a dutiful daughter, so I lean back and let Father scoot past me to exit the carriage.

He pushes the door open with enough force that the frame swings back and hits the carriage, making the glass rattle in its setting. The bellowing voice Father uses when most upset greets those on the other side of the small four walls I'm trapped within. "Excuse me. What is going on here? Do you not know who you have stopped?"

I pinch the bridge of my nose. *Ugh, the pompous attitude? Really, Father? You're a duke, but that doesn't change the fact that we're probably being held up by bandits.*

My hand drops from my face as I go back to watching Father and stopping myself from stepping down onto the dirt road to knock some sense into him before a bandit does. Father moves farther away from the carriage, and I keep my hand on the door, holding it open so I can hear more clearly what is being said.

"...All I have in my carriage is my daughter's dowry," Father states.

I can't hear what the bandit says, but when Father sputters again, I can't help but cover my smile. He's really selling this capable duke role, and again I wonder what he's going to do when I'm not here to help him navigate court life. I'm no expert, but Father only understands his ledgers, not the intricacies of relationships—something I've been studying since he brought me to court two years ago.

Father shouts, "You cannot. She is off to marry the prince of Rovia. You would dare endanger such a beneficial political alliance for our kingdom?"

Somebody gag me. I don't want to marry for an alliance. And I don't want to leave Lyriva either.

The bandit speaks, loud enough this time for me to hear. The tone of his voice intrigues me. "Then your daughter is welcome to marry one of my merry men, for today we are taking her dowry. You may relinquish it quietly and with ease, or we may tie you up and force you to hand over the dowry."

I don't hear what's said next as my mind races like one of Father's prized horses.

Rumors of Robin Hood and his merry men have infiltrated the court, many other noblemen having been robbed while riding the highways of the kingdom. There have also been whispers from the servants of poor, hungry families leaving for the woods and never returning from Sherwood Forest.

Maybe that's where all the good men have gone. They've turned into honorable outlaws who use their coins to quietly help the poor.

I'd be happy to marry an honorable outlaw who steals from the rich to feed the poor. He'd be better than the spineless boys of the court, because without Prince Alvor, there are no good noblemen left.

"She's going to be a princess!" Father shouts, his voice halting my contemplation.

Those words? They're the last straw.

I clench my teeth as I sit up, gripping the silk folds of my skirt in a tight fist as I throw the carriage door open. The glass panes don't rattle this time.

My calf-skin boots hit the dirt and I turn, staring down the men even as I smooth my skirts. I step toward Father, who's surrounded by hooded men dressed in leather and looking like they're part of the forest.

They're also holding weapons.

I force myself to take a deep breath through the tightness in my chest. I focus on Father and stare into his wide eyes. "I told you I do not want to marry Rovia's prince, Father. But you didn't listen to me. Take this as the sign it is—that I will not marry a man I have never met. No matter if it makes me a princess. I do not care for them. I'd rather marry one of these bandits, for at least they have honor, unlike you—riding away without telling a soul where I'm going. And for what? So you can avoid the king's suspicions? You don't even care that I'm heartbroken over Prince Alvor. So no. I will not leave Lyriva."

I can't help it. I stomp my foot, even though I know it makes me look like a child. But I am so tired of Father choosing things for me. Forcing me to be at court. Matchmaking me with rude noblemen, and now deciding I'm going to marry a prince.

I. Don't. Want. A. Prince.

There's clapping.

Why is there clapping?

My gaze shoots to the man who I assume is the ringleader of these bandits. He stands before Father, clapping as he stares at me through his mask.

Father turns to the bandit. "What are you doing?"

The man continues his applause. "Celebrating a woman who knows her mind, and who has the guts to speak it. You'd do well to listen to her, for she'll guide you well."

Heat floods my cheeks, and I stare at the ground. Then I realize what he has said, and I straighten my spine. I move my shoulders back and raise my chin, holding myself as the lady my governess taught me to be.

The man in the hood, who I'd bet my dowry is Robin Hood, moves until I can see him fully. "My lady, if you ever wish to fall in love with a man who will respect your opinions and feelings, I offer you any of my merry men. They would do well to have a woman with such spirit at their side."

My eyes rove over this bandit. Something about the way he stands is different, and he doesn't speak like any man I know. No man has ever guessed my dreams, let alone something I decided I wanted less than a minute ago. A stray curl falls against my face, and I brush it away before looking around. The bandits are masked, but they have handsome facial structures. One melts from the forest, and though he's hooded, a red curl falls across his forehead.

His hair reminds me of my friend Elisabeth, whose locks match that color. The set of the man's shoulders reminds me of her older brother, long dead, though I don't doubt he'd have just as broad shoulders and handsome facial features if he were a bandit.

Resolve grows within me.

"See, Father? These men understand me. So it's either me or the dowry. Give them the money, and I'll go home and choose who I want to marry from the local nobleman. Or, keep the money, and I'll run away with these bandits."

It's a trap, one I should feel bad for using, but after studying books on warfare, and learning the art of twisting my words from the court, what does he expect? I know my father, and there is no way the illustrious Duke Wessex will settle for a lowly nobleman as my future husband—not when he's lost the chance for me to wed a prince. Which means I'll get my pick from these fine bandits.

Maybe I should call them highwaymen instead of bandits. Sounds more romantic that way.

I'm startled when Robin Hood bows. "My lady. I'd be happy to send any of my men to marry you at your own home. I'm afraid the woods would be no place for a fine young woman with tender sensibilities."

My hands land on my hips, and I glare at this ridiculous man. "What happened to me knowing my own mind?" Anger simmers within me. "You know what. Forget it. I choose banditry."

I step toward the man with the shocking red hair peeking out from his hood and mask and loop my arm through his. "Come on, bandit. We're leaving."

My heeled boots stomp in the dirt as I pull the bandit with me into the trees without looking back.

Will I miss Father? Yes.

But what did he expect? Probably not for me to race into the forest with an unknown man.

But a girl can only take so much of court drama and a controlling, overprotective father. Sometimes she just wants an adventure and to fall in love with a highwayman.

Continue William and Marian's story by scanning here:

THANKS FOR READING!

Thank you so much for reading Alvor and Rowena's story.

If you enjoyed this book, please consider leaving a review or star rating on your favorite reviewing platforms.

What's happening in the kingdom of Rovia with Rowena's cousins? Find out in Book 2 of The Favored's Curse Series.

Charmed Beast: A Cinderella and Beauty and the Beast Retelling

ALSO BY M.K. FELIX

The Favored's Curse Series

Fairest Hunter

Lady Scarlett (A Companion Novella to Fairest Hunter)

Charmed Beast (2026)

Acknowledgments

Honestly, there are so many people I need to thank for helping get this book out into the world.

First and foremost, always and forever, is my Heavenly Father and my Savior Jesus Christ. Without Christ's enabling power I would have never finished this book or gotten through the Kickstarter or editing.

Next, my husband and children. They put up with a lot as I learned the ropes of Kickstarter, and worked to produce this book fast. I'm so grateful for their love and support, and for hearing how mom needs writing time way too often.

Writing a book is a team effort, and I'm so grateful for my team:

Robyn, thank you for helping me name characters, for your speedy beta reading, and assuring me it's fine to jump into the action only after they kiss.

Scarlett, thank you for answering my unending Kickstarter questions, your fearless friendship, and championing the story before you even read it.

Rachel and Moni, thank you for being my constant cheerleaders, late-night chat friends, and thank you for keeping me sane.

Anabelle, thank you for pointing out plot questions and making sure I did my backstory work. This story is so much stronger because of your help.

Ursi, Ashley, Isabelle, thank you for doing a quick beta read for me and reassuring me that you liked the book and it was good. Always need that support during those weeks when you're not sure what in the world you're doing.

Of course, Caitlin, my editor. You truly make my writing shine by reminding me where commas go, and how to use the right words. Thank you for working on this, even with everything else going on in your life.

Alicia, thanks for being an amazing proofreader and cheerleader. Your reaction messages were timely, and I love how hard you work to make sure my books are polished. You're awesome.

ABOUT THE AUTHOR

M.K. Felix writes clean, magical stories where fairy tales get fresh twists, romance stays swoony but sweet, and light always wins in the end. A lifelong book lover, she finally gave in to the call of storytelling three years ago and hasn't stopped writing since—especially tales where magic is rooted in light, inspired by her faith and her desire to share the light of Christ with the world.

When she's not twisting fairy tales together and writing romantasy, you'll find her chasing her two kids, laughing with her husband, or at church, recharging her soul. As a member of The Church of Jesus Christ of Latter-Day Saints, she writes with the hope of bringing wonder, faith, and hope to her readers.

With a bachelor's in Business Management and an associate degree in Project Management, she knows how to wrangle both spreadsheets and plot twists—but she'd always rather be in a world of enchanted forests, cursed princes, and rebels with a cause.

www.ingramcontent.com/pod-product-compliance
Lightning Source LLC
LaVergne TN
LVHW091249110826
845146LV00002BA/588